T0059441

A TIMELESS CHRISTMAS

A TIMELESS CHRISTMAS

A COLLECTION OF CLASSIC

STORIES AND POEMS

THOMAS NELSON

Since 1798

Editor's note: In order to preserve the authenticity of these works, many old, variant spellings of words have been maintained. We have made only minor adjustments to punctuation uses in order to improve readability.

Library of Congress Cataloging-in-Publication Data

Title: A timeless Christmas : a collection of classic stories and poems.
Description: [Nashville] : Thomas Nelson, [2020] | Summary: "This holiday season, give the readers in your life a beautiful collection of timeless Christmas stories and poems they will surely cherish for years to come"-- Provided by publisher.
Identifiers: LCCN 2020020609 (print) | LCCN 2020020610 (ebook) | ISBN 9780785238706 (hardcover) | ISBN 9780785238713 (epub) | ISBN 9780785238720 (downloadable audio)
Subjects: LCSH: Christmas--Literary collections. | Christmas stories. | Christmas poetry.
Classification: LCC PN6071.C6 T55 2020 (print) | LCC PN6071.C6 (ebook) | DDC 808.8/0334--dc23
LC record available at https://lccn.loc.gov/2020020609
LC ebook record available at https://lccn.loc.gov/2020020610

Printed in the United States of America
20 21 22 23 LSC 5 4 3 2 1

CONTENTS

CONTENTS

POEMS

STORIES AND SKETCHES

O. HENRY

1862-1910

THE GIFT OF THE MAGI

One dollar and eighty-seven cents. That was all. And sixty cents of it was in pennies. Pennies saved one and two at a time by bulldozing the grocer and the vegetable man and the butcher until one's cheeks burned with the silent imputation of parsimony that such close dealing implied. Three times Della counted it. One dollar and eighty-seven cents. And the next day would be Christmas.

There was clearly nothing to do but flop down on the shabby little couch and howl. So Della did it. Which instigates the moral reflection that life is made up of sobs, sniffles, and smiles, with sniffles predominating.

While the mistress of the home is gradually subsiding from the first stage to the second, take a look at the home. A furnished flat at $8 per week. It did not exactly beggar description, but it certainly had that word on the lookout for the mendicancy squad.

In the vestibule below was a letter-box into which no letter would go, and an electric button from which no mortal finger could coax a ring. Also appertaining thereunto was a card bearing the name "Mr. James Dillingham Young."

The "Dillingham" had been flung to the breeze during a former period of prosperity when its possessor was being paid $30 per week. Now, when the income was shrunk to $20, though, they were thinking seriously of contracting to a modest and unassuming D. But whenever Mr. James Dillingham Young came home and reached his flat above he was called "Jim" and greatly hugged by Mrs. James Dillingham Young, already introduced to you as Della. Which is all very good.

Della finished her cry and attended to her cheeks with the powder rag. She stood by the window and looked out dully at a gray cat walking a gray fence in a gray backyard. Tomorrow would be Christmas Day, and she had only $1.87 with which to buy Jim a present. She had been saving every penny she could for months, with this result. Twenty dollars a week doesn't go far. Expenses had been greater than she had calculated. They always are. Only $1.87 to buy a present for Jim. Her Jim. Many a happy hour she had spent planning for something nice for him. Something fine and rare and sterling—something just a little bit near to being worthy of the honor of being owned by Jim.

There was a pier glass between the windows of the room. Perhaps you have seen a pier glass in an $8 flat. A very thin and very agile person may, by observing his reflection in a rapid sequence of longitudinal strips, obtain a fairly accurate conception of his looks. Della, being slender, had mastered the art.

Suddenly she whirled from the window and stood before the glass. Her eyes were shining brilliantly, but her face had lost its color within twenty seconds. Rapidly she pulled down her hair and let it fall to its full length.

Now, there were two possessions of the James Dillingham Youngs in which they both took a mighty pride. One was Jim's gold watch that had been his father's and his grandfather's. The other was Della's hair. Had the queen of Sheba lived in the flat across the airshaft, Della would have let her hair hang out the window some day to dry just to depreciate Her Majesty's jewels and gifts. Had King Solomon been the janitor, with all his treasures piled up in the basement, Jim would have pulled out his watch every time he passed, just to see him pluck at his beard from envy.

So now Della's beautiful hair fell about her rippling and shining like a cascade of brown waters. It reached below her knee and made itself almost a garment for her. And then she did it up again nervously and quickly. Once she faltered for a minute and stood still while a tear or two splashed on the worn red carpet.

On went her old brown jacket; on went her old brown hat. With a whirl of skirts and with the brilliant sparkle still in her eyes, she fluttered out the door and down the stairs to the street.

Where she stopped the sign read: "Mme. Sofronie. Hair Goods of All Kinds." One flight up Della ran, and collected herself, panting. Madame, large, too white, chilly, hardly looked the "Sofronie."

"Will you buy my hair?" asked Della.

"I buy hair," said Madame. "Take yer hat off and let's have a sight at the looks of it."

Down rippled the brown cascade.

"Twenty dollars," said Madame, lifting the mass with a practiced hand.

"Give it to me quick," said Della.

Oh, and the next two hours tripped by on rosy wings. Forget the hashed metaphor. She was ransacking the stores for Jim's present.

She found it at last. It surely had been made for Jim and no one else. There was no other like it in any of the stores, and she had turned all of them inside out. It was a platinum fob chain simple and chaste in design, properly proclaiming its value by substance alone and not by meretricious ornamentation—as all good things should do. It was even worthy of The Watch. As soon as she saw it she knew that it must be Jim's. It was like him. Quietness and value—the description applied to both. Twenty-one dollars they took from her for it, and she hurried home with the 87 cents. With that chain on his watch Jim might be properly anxious about the time in any company. Grand as the watch was, he sometimes looked at it on the sly on account of the old leather strap that he used in place of a chain.

When Della reached home her intoxication gave way a little to prudence and reason. She got out her curling irons and lighted the gas and went to work repairing the ravages made by generosity added to love. Which is always a tremendous task, dear friends—a mammoth task.

Within forty minutes her head was covered with tiny, close-lying curls that made her look wonderfully like a truant schoolboy. She looked at her reflection in the mirror long, carefully, and critically.

"If Jim doesn't kill me," she said to herself, "before he takes a second look at me, he'll say I look like a Coney Island chorus girl. But what could I do—oh! what could I do with a dollar and eighty-seven cents?"

At seven o'clock the coffee was made and the frying pan was on the back of the stove hot and ready to cook the chops.

Jim was never late. Della doubled the fob chain in her hand and sat on the corner of the table near the door that he always entered. Then she heard his step on the stair away down on the first flight, and she turned white for just a moment. She had a habit of saying a little silent prayer about the simplest everyday things, and now she whispered: "Please God, make him think I am still pretty."

The door opened and Jim stepped in and closed it. He looked thin and very serious. Poor fellow, he was only twenty-two—and to be burdened with a family! He needed a new overcoat and he was without gloves.

Jim stopped inside the door, as immovable as a setter at the scent of quail. His eyes were fixed upon Della, and there was an expression in them that she could not read, and it terrified her. It was not anger, nor surprise, nor disapproval, nor horror, nor any of the sentiments that she had been prepared for. He simply stared at her fixedly with that peculiar expression on his face.

Della wriggled off the table and went for him.

"Jim, darling," she cried, "don't look at me

that way. I had my hair cut off and sold because I couldn't have lived through Christmas without giving you a present. It'll grow out again—you won't mind, will you? I just had to do it. My hair grows awfully fast. Say 'Merry Christmas!' Jim, and let's be happy. You don't know what a nice— what a beautiful, nice gift I've got for you."

"You've cut off your hair?" asked Jim, laboriously, as if he had not arrived at that patent fact yet even after the hardest mental labor.

"Cut it off and sold it," said Della. "Don't you like me just as well, anyhow? I'm me without my hair, ain't I?"

Jim looked about the room curiously.

"You say your hair is gone?" he said, with an air almost of idiocy.

"You needn't look for it," said Della. "It's sold, I tell you—sold and gone, too. It's Christmas Eve, boy. Be good to me, for it went for you. Maybe the hairs of my head were numbered," she went on with sudden serious sweetness, "but nobody could ever count my love for you. Shall I put the chops on, Jim?"

Out of his trance Jim seemed quickly to wake. He enfolded his Della. For ten seconds let us regard with discreet scrutiny some inconsequential object in the other direction. Eight dollars a week or a million a year—what is the difference? A mathematician or a wit would give you the wrong answer. The magi brought valuable gifts, but that was not among them. This dark assertion will be illuminated later on.

Jim drew a package from his overcoat pocket and threw it upon the table.

"Don't make any mistake, Dell," he said, "about me. I don't think there's anything in the way of a haircut or a shave or a shampoo that could make me like my girl any less. But if you'll unwrap that package you may see why you had me going a while at first."

White fingers and nimble tore at the string and paper. And then an ecstatic scream of joy; and then, alas! a quick feminine change to hysterical tears and wails, necessitating the immediate employment of all the comforting powers of the lord of the flat.

For there lay The Combs—the set of combs,

side and back, that Della had worshipped long in a Broadway window. Beautiful combs, pure tortoise shell, with jewelled rims—just the shade to wear in the beautiful vanished hair. They were expensive combs, she knew, and her heart had simply craved and yearned over them without the least hope of possession. And now, they were hers, but the tresses that should have adorned the coveted adornments were gone.

But she hugged them to her bosom, and at length she was able to look up with dim eyes and a smile and say: "My hair grows so fast, Jim!"

And then Della leaped up like a little singed cat and cried, "Oh, oh!"

Jim had not yet seen his beautiful present. She held it out to him eagerly upon her open palm. The dull precious metal seemed to flash with a reflection of her bright and ardent spirit.

"Isn't it a dandy, Jim? I hunted all over town to find it. You'll have to look at the time a hundred times a day now. Give me your watch. I want to see how it looks on it."

Instead of obeying, Jim tumbled down on the

couch and put his hands under the back of his head and smiled.

"Dell," said he, "let's put our Christmas presents away and keep 'em a while. They're too nice to use just at present. I sold the watch to get the money to buy your combs. And now suppose you put the chops on."

The magi, as you know, were wise men—wonderfully wise men—who brought gifts to the Babe in the manger. They invented the art of giving Christmas presents. Being wise, their gifts were no doubt wise ones, possibly bearing the privilege of exchange in case of duplication. And here I have lamely related to you the uneventful chronicle of two foolish children in a flat who most unwisely sacrificed for each other the greatest treasures of their house. But in a last word to the wise of these days let it be said that of all who give gifts these two were the wisest. Of all who give and receive gifts, such as they are wisest. Everywhere they are wisest. They are the magi.

L. M. MONTGOMERY

1874-1942

THE JOSEPHS' CHRISTMAS

The month before Christmas was always the most exciting and mysterious time in the Joseph household. Such scheming and planning, such putting of curly heads together in corners, such counting of small hoards, such hiding and smuggling of things out of sight, as went on among the little Josephs!

There were a good many of them, and very few of the pennies; hence the reason for so much contriving and consulting. From fourteen-year-old Mollie down to four-year-old Lennie there were eight small Josephs in all in the little log house on the prairie; so that when each little Joseph wanted to give a Christmas box to each of the other little Josephs, and something to Father and Mother Joseph besides, it is no wonder that they had to cudgel their small brains for ways and means thereof.

Father and Mother were always discreetly

blind and silent through December. No questions were asked no matter what queer things were done. Many secret trips to the little store at the railway station two miles away were ignored, and no little Joseph was called to account because he or she looked terribly guilty when somebody suddenly came into the room. The air was simply charged with secrets.

Sister Mollie was the grand repository of these; all the little Josephs came to her for advice and assistance. It was Mollie who for troubled small brothers and sisters did such sums in division as this: How can I get a ten-cent present for Emmy and a fifteen-cent one for Jimmy out of eighteen cents? Or, how can seven sticks of candy be divided among eight people so that each shall have one? It was Mollie who advised regarding the purchase of ribbon and crepe paper. It was Mollie who put the finishing touches to most of the little gifts. In short, all through December Mollie was weighed down under an avalanche of responsibility. It speaks volumes for her sagacity and skill that she never got things mixed up or made any such terrible mistake as letting one little Joseph find out what another was going to give him. "Dead" secrecy was the keystone of all plans and confidences.

During this particular December the planning and contriving had been more difficult and the results less satisfactory than usual. The Josephs were poor at any time, but this winter they were poorer than ever. The crops had failed in the summer, and as a consequence the family were, as Jimmy said, "on short commons." But they made the brave best of their small resources, and on Christmas Eve every little Joseph went to bed with a clear conscience, for was there not on the corner table in the kitchen a small mountain of tiny—sometimes very tiny—gifts labelled with the names of recipients and givers, and worth their weight in gold if love and good wishes count for anything?

It was beginning to snow when the small small Josephs went to bed, and when the big small Josephs climbed the stairs it was snowing thickly. Mr. and Mrs. Joseph sat before the fire and listened to the wind howling about the house.

"I'm glad I'm not driving over the prairie to-night," said Mr. Joseph. "It's quite a storm. I hope it will be fine tomorrow, for the children's sake. They've set their hearts on having a sleigh ride, and it will be too bad if they can't have it when it's about all the Christmas they'll have this year. Mary, this is the first Christmas since we came west that we couldn't afford some little extras for them, even if 'twas only a box of nuts and candy."

Mrs. Joseph sighed over Jimmy's worn jacket which she was mending. Then she smiled.

"Never mind, John. Things will be better next Christmas, we'll hope. The children will not mind, bless their hearts. Look at all the little knick-knacks they've made for each other. Last week when I was over at Taunton, Mr. Fisher had his store all 'gayified up,' as Jim says, with Christmas presents. I did feel that I'd ask nothing better than to go in and buy all the lovely things I wanted, just for once, and give them to the children tomorrow morning. They've never had anything really nice for Christmas. But there! We've all got each other and good health and spirits, and a Christmas wouldn't be much without those if we had all the presents in the world."

Mr. Joseph nodded.

"That's so. I don't want to grumble; but I tell you I did want to get Maggie a 'real live doll,' as she calls it. She never has had anything but home-made dolls, and that small heart of hers is set on a real one. There was one at Fisher's store today—a big beauty with real hair, and eyes that opened and shut. Just fancy Maggie's face if she saw such a Christmas box as that tomorrow morning."

"Don't let's fancy it," laughed Mrs. Joseph, "it is only aggravating. Talking of candy reminds me that I made a big plateful of taffy for the children today. It's all the 'Christmassy' I could give them. I'll get it out and put it on the table along with the children's presents. That can't be someone at the door!"

"It is, though," said Mr. Joseph as he strode to the door and flung it open.

Two snowed-up figures were standing on the porch. As they stepped in, the Josephs recognized one of them as Mr. Ralston, a wealthy merchant in a small town fifteen miles away.

"Late hour for callers, isn't it?" said Mr. Ralston. "The fact is, our horse has about given out, and the storm is so bad that we can't proceed. This is my wife, and we are on our way to spend Christmas with my brother's family at Lindsay. Can you take us in for the night, Mr. Joseph?"

"Certainly, and welcome!" exclaimed Mr. Joseph heartily, "if you don't mind a shakedown by the kitchen fire for the night. My, Mrs. Ralston," as his wife helped her off with her things, "but you are snowed up! I'll see to putting your horse away, Mr. Ralston. This way, if you please."

When the two men came stamping into the house again Mrs. Ralston and Mrs. Joseph were sitting at the fire, the former with a steaming hot cup of tea in her hand. Mr. Ralston put the big basket he was carrying down on a bench in the corner.

"Thought I'd better bring our Christmas flummery in," he said. "You see, Mrs. Joseph, my brother has a big family, so we are taking them a lot of Santa Claus stuff. Mrs. Ralston packed this basket, and goodness knows what she put in it, but she half cleaned out my store. The eyes of the Lindsay youngsters will dance tomorrow—that is, if we ever get there."

Mrs. Joseph gave a little sigh in spite of herself, and looked wistfully at the heap of gifts on the corner table. How meagre and small they did look, to be sure, beside that bulgy basket with its cover suggestively tied down.

Mrs. Ralston looked too.

"Santa Claus seems to have visited you already," she said with a smile.

The Josephs laughed.

"Our Santa Claus is somewhat out of pocket this year," said Mr. Joseph frankly. "Those are the little things the small folks here have made for each other. They've been a month at it, and I'm always kind of relieved when Christmas is over and there are no more mysterious doings. We're in such cramped quarters here that you can't move without stepping on somebody's secret."

A shakedown was spread in the kitchen for

the unexpected guests, and presently the Ralstons found themselves alone. Mrs. Ralston went over to the Christmas table and looked at the little gifts half tenderly and half pityingly.

"They're not much like the contents of our basket, are they?" she said, as she touched the calendar Jimmie had made for Mollie out of cardboard and autumn leaves and grasses.

"Just what I was thinking," returned her husband, "and I was thinking of something else, too. I've a notion that I'd like to see some of the things in our basket right here on this table."

"I'd like to see them all," said Mrs. Ralston promptly. "Let's just leave them here, Edward. Roger's family will have plenty of presents without them, and for that matter we can send them ours when we go back home."

"Just as you say," agreed Mr. Ralston. "I like the idea of giving the small folk of this household a rousing good Christmas for once. They're poor I know, and I dare say pretty well pinched this year like most of the farmers hereabout after the crop failure."

Mrs. Ralston untied the cover of the big basket. Then the two of them, moving as stealthily as if engaged in a burglary, transferred the contents to the table. Mr. Ralston got out a small pencil and a note book, and by dint of comparing the names attached to the gifts on the table they managed to divide theirs up pretty evenly among the little Josephs.

When all was done Mrs. Ralston said, "Now, I'm going to spread that tablecloth carelessly over the table. We will be going before daylight, probably, and in the hurry of getting off I hope that Mr. and Mrs. Joseph will not notice the difference till we're gone."

It fell out as Mrs. Ralston had planned. The dawn broke fine and clear over a vast white world. Mr. and Mrs. Joseph were early astir; breakfast for the storm-stayed travellers was cooked and eaten by lamplight; then the horse and sleigh were brought to the door and Mr. Ralston carried out his empty basket.

"I expect the trail will be heavy," he said, "but I guess we'd get to Lindsay in time for dinner, anyway. Much obliged for your kindness, Mr. Joseph. When you and Mrs. Joseph come to town we shall hope to have a chance to return it. Good-bye and a merry Christmas to you all."

When Mrs. Joseph went back to the kitchen her eyes fell on the heaped-up table in the corner.

"Why-y!" she said, and snatched off the cover.

One look she gave, and then this funny little mother began to cry; but they were happy tears. Mr. Joseph came too, and looked and whistled.

There really seemed to be everything on that table that the hearts of children could desire— three pairs of skates, a fur cap and collar, a dainty workbasket, half a dozen gleaming new books, a writing desk, a roll of stuff that looked like a new dress, a pair of fur-topped kid gloves just Mollie's size, and a china cup and saucer. All these were to be seen at the first glance; and in one corner of the table was a big box filled with candies and nuts and raisins, and in the other a doll with curling golden hair and brown eyes, dressed in "real" clothes and with all her wardrobe in a trunk beside her. Pinned to her dress was a leaf from

Mr. Ralston's notebook with Maggie's name written on it.

"Well, this is Christmas with a vengeance," said Mr. Joseph.

"The children will go wild with delight," said his wife happily.

They pretty nearly did when they all came scrambling down the stairs a little later. Such a Christmas had never been known in the Joseph household before. Maggie clasped her doll with shining eyes, Mollie looked at the workbasket that her housewifely little heart had always longed for, studious Jimmy beamed over the books, and Ted and Hal whooped with delight over the skates. And as for the big box of good things, why, everybody appreciated that. That Christmas was one to date from in that family.

I'm glad to be able to say, too, that even in the heyday of their delight and surprise over their wonderful presents, the little Josephs did not forget to appreciate the gifts they had prepared for each other. Mollie thought her calendar just too pretty for anything, and Jimmy was sure the new red mittens which Maggie had knitted for him with her own chubby wee fingers, were the very nicest, gayest mittens a boy had ever worn.

Mrs. Joseph's taffy was eaten too. Not a scrap of it was left. As Ted said loyally, "It was just as good as the candy in the box and had more 'chew' to it besides."

THE OSBORNES' CHRISTMAS

Cousin Myra had come to spend Christmas at "The Firs," and all the junior Osbornes were ready to stand on their heads with delight. Darby—whose real name was Charles—did it, because he was only eight, and at eight you have no dignity to keep up. The others, being older, couldn't.

But the fact of Christmas itself awoke no great enthusiasm in the hearts of the junior Osbornes. Frank voiced their opinion of it the day after Cousin Myra had arrived. He was sitting on the table with his hands in his pockets and a cynical sneer on his face. At least, Frank flattered himself that it was cynical. He knew that Uncle Edgar was said to wear a cynical sneer, and Frank admired Uncle Edgar very much and imitated him in every possible way. But to you and me it would have looked just as it did to Cousin Myra—a very dis-contented and unbecoming scowl.

"I'm awfully glad to see you, Cousin Myra,"

explained Frank carefully, "and your being here may make some things worth while. But Christmas is just a bore—a regular bore."

That was what Uncle Edgar called things that didn't interest him, so that Frank felt pretty sure of his word. Nevertheless, he wondered uncomfortably what made Cousin Myra smile so queerly.

"Why, how dreadful!" she said brightly. "I thought all boys and girls looked upon Christmas as the very best time in the year."

"We don't," said Frank gloomily. "It's just the same old thing year in and year out. We know just exactly what is going to happen. We even know pretty well what presents we are going to get. And Christmas Day itself is always the same. We'll get up in the morning, and our stockings will be full of things, and half of them we don't want. Then there's dinner. It's always so poky. And all the uncles and aunts come to dinner—just the same old crowd, every year, and they say just the same things. Aunt Desda always says, 'Why, Frankie, how you have grown!' She knows I hate to be called Frankie. And after dinner they'll sit round and talk the rest of the day, and that's all. Yes, I call Christmas a nuisance."

"There isn't a single bit of fun in it," said Ida discontentedly.

"Not a bit!" said the twins, both together, as they always said things.

"There's lots of candy," said Darby stoutly. He rather liked Christmas, although he was ashamed to say so before Frank.

Cousin Myra smothered another of those queer smiles.

"You've had too much Christmas, you Osbornes," she said seriously. "It has palled on your taste, as all good things will if you overdo them. Did you ever try giving Christmas to somebody else?"

The Osbornes looked at Cousin Myra doubtfully. They didn't understand.

"We always send presents to all our cousins," said Frank hesitatingly. "That's a bore, too. They've all got so many things already it's no end of bother to think of something new."

"That isn't what I mean," said Cousin Myra. "How much Christmas do you suppose those little Rolands down there in the hollow have? Or Sammy Abbott with his lame back? Or French Joe's family over the hill? If you have too much Christmas, why don't you give some to them?"

The Osbornes looked at each other. This was a new idea.

"How could we do it?" asked Ida.

Whereupon they had a consultation. Cousin Myra explained her plan, and the Osbornes grew enthusiastic over it. Even Frank forgot that he was supposed to be wearing a cynical sneer.

"I move we do it, Osbornes," said he.

"If Father and Mother are willing," said Ida.

"Won't it be jolly!" exclaimed the twins.

"Well, rather," said Darby scornfully. He did not mean to be scornful. He had heard Frank saying the same words in the same tone, and thought it signified approval.

Cousin Myra had a talk with Father and Mother Osborne that night, and found them heartily in sympathy with her plans.

For the next week the Osbornes were agog with excitement and interest. At first Cousin Myra made the suggestions, but their enthusiasm soon outstripped her, and they thought out things for themselves. Never did a week pass so quickly. And the Osbornes had never had such fun, either.

Christmas morning there was not a single present given or received at "The Firs" except those which Cousin Myra and Mr. and Mrs. Osborne gave to each other. The junior Osbornes had asked that the money which their parents had planned to spend in presents for them be given to them the previous week; and given it was, without a word.

The uncles and aunts arrived in due time, but not with them was the junior Osbornes' concern. They were the guests of Mr. and Mrs. Osborne. The junior Osbornes were having a Christmas dinner party of their own. In the small dining room a table was spread and loaded with good things. Ida and the twins cooked that dinner all by themselves. To be sure, Cousin Myra had helped some, and Frank and Darby had stoned all the raisins and helped pull the home-made candy; and all together they had decorated the small dining room royally with Christmas greens.

Then their guests came. First, all the little Rolands from the Hollow arrived—seven in all, with very red, shining faces and not a word to say for themselves, so shy were they. Then came a troop from French Joe's—four black-eyed lads, who never knew what shyness meant. Frank drove down to the village in the cutter and brought lame Sammy back with him, and soon after the last guest arrived—little Tillie Mather, who was Miss Rankin's "orphan 'sylum girl" from over the road. Everybody knew that Miss Rankin never kept Christmas. She did not believe in it, she said, but she did not prevent Tillie from going to the Osbornes' dinner party.

Just at first the guests were a little stiff and unsocial; but they soon got acquainted, and so jolly was Cousin Myra—who had her dinner with the children in preference to the grown-ups—and so friendly the junior Osbornes, that all stiffness vanished. What a merry dinner it was! What peals of laughter went up, reaching to the big dining room across the hall, where the grown-ups sat in rather solemn state. And how those guests did eat and frankly enjoy the good things before them! How nicely they all behaved, even to the French Joes! Myra had secretly been a little dubious about those four mischievous-looking lads, but their manners were quite flawless. Mrs. French Joe had been drilling them for three days—ever since they had been invited to "de Chrismus dinner at de beeg house."

After the merry dinner was over, the junior Osbornes brought in a Christmas tree, loaded with presents. They had bought them with the money that Mr. and Mrs. Osborne had meant for their own presents, and a splendid assortment they were. All the French Joe boys got a pair of skates apiece, and Sammy a set of beautiful books, and Tillie was made supremely happy with a big wax doll. Every little Roland got just what his or her small heart had been longing for. Besides, there were nuts and candies galore.

Then Frank hitched up his pony again, but

this time into a great pung sleigh, and the junior Osbornes took their guests for a sleigh-drive, chaperoned by Cousin Myra. It was just dusk when they got back, having driven the Rolands and the French Joes and Sammy and Tillie to their respective homes.

"This has been the jolliest Christmas I ever spent," said Frank, emphatically.

"I thought we were just going to give the others a good time, but it was they who gave it to us," said Ida.

"Weren't the French Joes jolly?" giggled the twins. "Such cute speeches as they would make!"

"Me and Teddy Roland are going to be chums after this," announced Darby. "He's an inch taller than me, but I'm wider."

That night Frank and Ida and Cousin Myra had a little talk after the smaller Osbornes had been haled off to bed.

"We're not going to stop with Christmas, Cousin Myra," said Frank, at the end of it. "We're just going to keep on through the year. We've never had such a delightful old Christmas before."

"You've learned the secret of happiness," said Cousin Myra gently.

And the Osbornes understood what she meant.

ELIZABETH HARRISON

1849-1927

LITTLE GRETCHEN AND THE WOODEN SHOE

Once upon a time, a long time ago, far away across the great ocean, in a country called Germany, there could be seen a small log hut on the edge of a great forest, whose fir trees extended for miles and miles to the north. This little house, made of heavy hewn logs, had but one room in it. A rough pine door gave entrance to this room, and a small square window admitted the light. At the back of the house was built an old-fashioned stone chimney, out of which in winter curled a thin, blue smoke, showing that there was not very much fire within.

Small as the house was, it was large enough for the two people who lived in it. I want to tell you a story today about these two people. One was an old gray-haired woman, so old that the little children of the village, nearly half a mile away, often wondered whether she had come into the world with the huge mountains and the giant fir trees, which stood like giants back of her small hut. Her face was wrinkled all over with deep lines, which, if the children could only have read aright, would have told them of many years of cheerful, happy, self-sacrifice; of loving, anxious, watching beside sick-beds; of quiet endurance of pain, of many a day of hunger and cold, and of a thousand deeds of unselfish love for other people; but, of course, they could not read this strange handwriting. They only knew that she was old and wrinkled, and that she stooped as she walked. None of them seemed to fear her, for her smile was always cheerful, and she had a kindly word for each of them if they chanced to meet her on her way to and from the village. With this old, old woman lived a very little girl. So bright and happy was she that the travellers who passed by the lonesome little house on the edge of the forest often thought of a sunbeam as they saw her. These two people were known in the village as Granny Goodyear and Little Gretchen.

The winter had come and the frost had snapped off many of the smaller branches of the pine trees in the forest. Gretchen and her granny were up by daybreak each morning. After their simple breakfast of oatmeal, Gretchen would run to the little closet and fetch Granny's old woolen shawl, which seemed almost as old as Granny herself. Gretchen always claimed the right to put the shawl over Granny's head, even though she had to climb onto the wooden bench to do it. After carefully pinning it under Granny's chin, she gave her a good-bye kiss, and Granny started out for her morning's work in the forest. This work was nothing more nor less than the gathering up of the twigs and branches which the autumn winds and winter frosts had thrown upon the ground. These were carefully gathered into a large bundle which Granny tied together with a strong linen band. She then managed to lift the bundle to her shoulder and trudged off to the village with it. Here she sold the fagots for kindling wood to the people of the village. Sometimes she would get only a few pence each day, and sometimes a dozen or more, but on this money little Gretchen and she managed to live; they had their home, and the forest kindly furnished the wood for the fire which kept them warm in winter.

In the summer time Granny had a little garden at the back of the house, where she raised, with little Gretchen's help, a few potatoes and turnips and onions. These she carefully stored away for winter use. To this meagre supply, the pennies, gained by selling the twigs from the forest, added the oatmeal for Gretchen and a little black coffee for Granny. Meat was a thing they never thought of having. It cost too much money. Still, Granny and Gretchen were very happy, because they loved each other dearly. Sometimes Gretchen would be left alone all day long in the hut, because Granny would have some work to do in the village after selling her bundle of sticks and twigs. It was during these long days that little Gretchen had taught herself to sing the song which the wind sang to the pine branches. In the summer time she learned the chirp and twitter of the birds, until her voice might almost be mistaken for a bird's voice, she learned to dance as the swaying shadows did, and even to talk to the stars which shone through the little square window when Granny came home late or too tired to talk.

Sometimes, when the weather was fine, or her Granny had an extra bundle of knitted stockings to take to the village, she would let little Gretchen go along with her. It chanced that one of these trips to the town came just the week before Christmas, and Gretchen's eyes were delighted by the sight of the lovely Christmas trees which stood in the window of the village store. It seemed to her that she would never tire of looking at the knit dolls, the woolly lambs, the little wooden shops with their queer, painted men and women in them, and all the other fine things. She had never owned a plaything in her whole life; therefore, toys which you and I would not think much of seemed to her very beautiful.

That night, after their supper of baked potatoes was over, and little Gretchen had cleared away the dishes and swept up the hearth, because Granny dear was so tired, she brought her own little wooden stool and placed it very near Granny's feet and sat down upon it, folding her hands on her lap. Granny knew that this meant that she wanted to be told about something, so she smilingly laid away the large Bible which she had been reading, and took up her knitting, which was as much as to say: "Well, Gretchen, dear, Granny is ready to listen."

"Granny," said Gretchen slowly, "it's almost Christmas time, isn't it?"

"Yes, dearie," said Granny, "only five days more now," and then she sighed, but little Gretchen was so happy that she did not notice Granny's sigh.

"What do you think, Granny, I'll get this Christmas?" said she, looking up eagerly into Granny's face.

"Ah, child, child," said Granny, shaking her head, "you'll have no Christmas this year. We are too poor for that."

"Oh, but Granny," interrupted little Gretchen, "think of all the beautiful toys we saw in the village today. Surely Santa Claus has sent enough for every little child."

"Ah, dearie, those toys are for people who can

pay for them, and we have no money to spend for Christmas toys."

"Well, Granny," said Gretchen, "perhaps some of the little children who live in the great house on the hill at the other end of the village, will be willing to share some of their toys with me. They will be glad to give some to a little girl who has none."

"Dear child, dear child," said Granny, leaning forward and stroking the soft, shiny hair of the little girl, "your heart is full of love. You would be glad to bring a Christmas to every child; but their heads are so full of what they are going to get that they forget all about anybody else but themselves." Then she sighed and shook her head.

"Well, Granny," said Gretchen, her bright, happy tone of voice growing a little less joyous, "perhaps the dear Santa Claus will show some of the village children how to make presents that do not cost money, and some of them may surprise me Christmas morning with a present. And, Granny, dear," added she, springing up from her low stool, "can't I gather some of the pine branches and take them to the old sick man who lives in the house by the mill, so that he can have the sweet smell of our forest in his room all Christmas day?"

"Yes, dearie," said Granny, "you may do what you can to make the Christmas bright and happy, but you must not expect any present yourself."

"Oh, but, Granny," said little Gretchen, her face brightening, "you forgot all about the shining Christmas angels, who came down to earth and sang their wonderful song the night the beautiful Christ-Child was born! They are so loving and good that *they* will not forget any little child. I shall ask my dear stars tonight to tell them of us. You know," she added, with a look of relief, "the stars are so very high that they must know the angels quite well as they come and go with their messages from the loving God."

Granny sighed as she half whispered. "Poor child, poor child!" but Gretchen threw her arm around Granny's neck and gave her a hearty kiss, saying as she did so: "Oh, Granny, Granny, you don't talk to the stars often enough, else you would not be sad at Christmas time." Then she danced all around the room, whirling her little skirts about her to show Granny how the wind had made the snow dance that day. She looked so droll and funny that Granny forgot her cares and worries and laughed with little Gretchen over her new snow dance. The days passed on and the morning before Christmas Eve came. Gretchen having tidied up the little room—for Granny had taught her to be a careful little housewife—was off to the forest, singing a birdlike song, almost as happy and free as the birds themselves. She was very busy that day preparing a surprise for Granny. First, however, she gathered the most beautiful of the fir branches within her reach to take the next morning to the old sick man who lived by the mill.

The day was all too short for the happy little girl. When Granny came trudging wearily home that night, she found the frame of the doorway covered with green pine branches.

"It is to welcome you, Granny! It is to welcome you!" cried Gretchen. "Our dear old home wanted to give you a Christmas welcome. Don't you see, the branches of the evergreen make it look as if it were smiling all over, and it is trying to say, 'A happy Christmas to you, Granny.'"

Granny laughed and kissed the little girl, as they opened the door and went in together. Here was a new surprise for Granny. The four posts of the wooden bed, which stood in one corner of the room, had been trimmed by the busy little fingers, with smaller and more flexible branches of the pine trees. A small bouquet of red mountain ash berries stood at each side of the fireplace, and these, together with the trimmed posts of the bed, gave the plain old room quite a festive look. Gretchen laughed and clapped her hands and danced about until the house seemed full of music to poor, tired Granny, whose heart had been sad as she turned toward their home that night, thinking of the disappointment that must come to loving little Gretchen the next morning.

After supper was over little Gretchen drew her stool up to Granny's side, and laying her soft, little hands on Granny's knee asked to be told once again the story of the coming of the Christ-Child;

how the night that he was born the beautiful angels had sung their wonderful song, and how the whole sky had become bright with a strange and glorious light, never seen by the people of earth before. Gretchen had heard the story many, many times before, but she never grew tired of it, and now that Christmas Eve had come again, the happy little child wanted to hear it once more.

When Granny had finished telling it the two sat quiet and silent for a little while thinking it over; then Granny rose and said that it was time for her to go to bed. She slowly took off her heavy wooden shoes, such as are worn in that country, and placed them beside the hearth. Gretchen looked thoughtfully at them for a minute or two, and then she said, "Granny, don't you think that *somebody* in all this wide world will think of us tonight?"

"Nay, Gretchen, I do not think any one will."

"Well, then, Granny," said Gretchen, "the Christmas angels will, I know; so I am going to take one of your wooden shoes and put it on the windowsill outside, so that they may see it as they pass by. I am sure the stars will tell the Christmas angels where the shoe is."

"Ah, you foolish, foolish child," said Granny, "you are only getting ready for a disappointment. Tomorrow morning there will be nothing whatever in the shoe. I can tell you that now."

But little Gretchen would not listen. She only shook her head and cried out: "Ah, Granny, you do not talk enough to the stars." With this she seized the shoe, and opening the door, hurried out to place it on the windowsill. It was very dark without and something soft and cold seemed to gently kiss her hair and face. Gretchen knew by this that it was snowing, and she looked up to the sky, anxious to see if the stars were in sight, but a strong wind was tumbling the dark, heavy snow-clouds about and had shut away all else.

"Never mind," said Gretchen softly to herself, "the stars are up there, even if I can't see them, and the Christmas angels do not mind snow storms."

Just then a rough wind went sweeping by the little girl, whispering something to her which she could not understand, and then it made a sudden rush up to the snow clouds and parted them, so that the deep mysterious sky appeared beyond, and shining down out of the midst of it was Gretchen's favorite star.

"Ah, little star, little star!" said the child, laughing aloud. "I knew you were there, though I could not see you. Will you whisper to the Christmas angels as they come by that little Gretchen wants so very much to have a Christmas gift tomorrow morning, if they have one to spare, and that she has put one of Granny's shoes upon the windowsill for it?"

A moment more and the little girl, standing on tiptoe, had reached the windowsill and placed the shoe upon it, and was back again in the house beside Granny and the warm fire.

The two went quietly to bed, and that night as little Gretchen knelt to pray to the Heavenly Father, she thanked him for having sent the Christ-Child into the world to teach all mankind to be loving and unselfish, and in a few minutes she was sleeping, dreaming of the Christmas angels.

The next morning, very early, even before the

sun was up, little Gretchen was awakened by the sound of sweet music coming from the village. She listened for a moment and then she knew that the choir boys were singing the Christmas carols in the open air of the village street. She sprang up out of bed and began to dress herself as quickly as possible, singing as she dressed. While Granny was slowly putting on her clothes, little Gretchen having finished dressing herself, unfastened the door and hurried out to see what the Christmas angels had left in the old wooden shoe.

The white snow covered everything—trees, stumps, roads, and pastures—until the whole world looked like fairy land. Gretchen climbed up on a large stone which was beneath the window and carefully lifted down the wooden shoe. The snow tumbled off of it in a shower over the little girl's hands, but she did not heed that; she ran hurriedly back into the house, putting her hand into the toe of the shoe as she ran.

"Oh, Granny, Granny!" she exclaimed. "You did not believe the Christmas angels would think about us, but see, they have, they have! Here is a dear little bird nestled down in the toe of your shoe! Oh, isn't he beautiful?"

Granny came forward and looked at what the child was holding lovingly in her hand. There she saw a tiny chick-a-dee, whose wing was evidently broken by the rough and boisterous winds of the night before, and who had taken shelter in the safe, dry toe of the old wooden shoe. She gently took the little bird out of Gretchen's hands, and skilfully bound his broken wing to his side, so that he need not hurt himself trying to fly with it. Then she showed Gretchen how to make a nice warm nest for the little stranger, close beside the fire and when their breakfast was ready, she let Gretchen feed the little bird with a few moist crumbs.

Later in the day Gretchen carried the fresh, green boughs to the old sick man by the mill, and on her way home stopped to enjoy the Christmas toys of some other children that she knew, never once wishing they were hers. When she reached home she found that the little bird had gone to sleep. Soon, however, he opened his eyes and stretched his head up, saying just as plain as a bird can say: "Now, my new friends, I want you to give me something more to eat." Gretchen gladly fed him again, and then, holding him in her lap, she softly and gently stroked his gray feathers until the little creature seemed to lose all fear of her. That evening Granny taught her a Christmas hymn and told her another beautiful Christmas story. Then Gretchen made up a funny little story to tell the birdie. He winked his eyes and turned his head from side to side in such a droll fashion that Gretchen laughed until the tears came.

As Granny and she got ready for bed that night, Gretchen put her arms softly around Granny's neck, and whispered: "What a beautiful Christmas we have had today, Granny. Is there anything more lovely in all the world than Christmas?"

"Nay, child, nay," said Granny, "not to such loving hearts as yours."

THE LEGEND OF THE CHRIST CHILD

A Story for Christmas Eve

I want to tell you to-night a story which has been told to little children in Germany for many hundreds of years.

Once upon a time, a long, long time ago, on the night before Christmas, a little child was wandering all alone through the streets of a great city. There were many people on the street, fathers and mothers, sisters and brothers, uncles and aunts, and even gray-haired grandfathers and grandmothers, all of whom were hurrying home with bundles of presents for each other and for their little ones. Fine carriages rolled by, express wagons rattled past, even old carts were pressed into service, and all things seemed in a hurry, and glad with expectation of the coming Christmas morning.

From some of the windows bright lights were already beginning to stream until it was almost as bright as day. But the little child seemed to have no home, and wandered about listlessly from street to street. No one took any notice of him, except perhaps Jack Frost, who bit his bare toes and made the ends of his fingers tingle. The north wind, too, seemed to notice the child, for it blew against him and pierced his ragged garments through and through, causing him to shiver with cold. Home after home he passed, looking with longing eyes through the windows, in upon the glad, happy children, most of whom were helping to trim the Christmas trees for the coming morrow.

"Surely," said the child to himself, "where there is so much gladness and happiness, some of it may be for me." So with timid steps he approached a large and handsome house. Through the windows he could see a tall and stately Christmas tree already lighted. Many presents hung upon it. Its green boughs were trimmed with gold and silver ornaments. Slowly he climbed up the broad steps and gently rapped at the door. It was opened by a large man-servant. He had a kindly face, although his voice was deep and gruff. He looked at the little child for a moment, then sadly shook his head and said, "Go down off the steps. There is no room here for such as you." He looked sorry as he spoke; possibly he remembered his own little ones at home, and was glad that they were not out in this cold and bitter night. Through the open door a bright light shone, and the warm air, filled with the fragrance of the Christmas pine, rushed out from the inner room and greeted the little wanderer with a kiss. As the child turned back into the cold and darkness, he wondered why the footman had spoken thus, for surely, thought he, those little children would love to have another companion join them in their joyous Christmas festival. But the little children inside did not even know that he had knocked at the door.

The street grew colder and darker as the child passed on. He went sadly forward, saying to himself, "Is there no one in all this great city who will share the Christmas with me?" Farther and farther down the street he wandered, to where the homes were not so large and beautiful. There seemed to be little children inside of nearly all the houses. They were dancing and frolicking about.

Christmas trees could be seen in nearly every window, with beautiful dolls and trumpets and picture-books and balls and tops and other dainty toys hung upon them. In one window the child noticed a little lamb made of soft, white wool. Around its neck was tied a red ribbon. It had evidently been hung on the tree for one of the children. The little stranger stopped before this window and looked long and earnestly at the beautiful things inside, but most of all was he drawn toward the white lamb. At last, creeping up to the window-pane, he gently tapped upon it. A little girl came to the window and looked out into the dark street where the snow had now begun to fall. She saw the child, but she only frowned and shook her head and said, "Go away and come some other time. We are too busy to take care of you now." Back into the dark, cold street he turned again. The wind was whirling past him and seemed to say, "Hurry on, hurry on, we have no time to stop. 'Tis Christmas Eve and everybody is in a hurry to-night."

Again and again the little child rapped softly

at door or window-pane. At each place he was refused admission. One mother feared he might have some ugly disease which her darlings would catch; another father said he had only enough for his own children, and none to spare for beggar brats. Still another told him to go home where he belonged, and not to trouble other folks.

The hours passed; later grew the night, and colder blew the wind, and darker seemed the street. Farther and farther the little one wandered. There was scarcely any one left upon the street by this time, and the few who remained did not seem to see the child, when suddenly ahead of him, there appeared a bright, single ray of light. It shone through the darkness into the child's eyes. He looked up smilingly, and said, "I will go where the small light beckons, perhaps they will share their Christmas with me."

Hurrying past all the other houses he soon reached the end of the street and went straight up to the window from which the light was streaming. It was a poor, little, low house, but the child cared not for that. The light seemed still to call him in. From what do you suppose the light came? Nothing but a tallow candle which had been placed in an old cup with a broken handle, in the window, as a glad token of Christmas Eve. There was neither curtain nor shade to the small, square window, and as the little child looked in he saw standing upon a neat, wooden table a branch of a Christmas tree. The room was plainly furnished, but it was very clean. Near the fireplace sat a lovely faced mother with a little two-year-old on her knee and an older child beside her. The two children were looking into their mother's face and listening to a story. She must have been telling them a Christmas story, I think. A few bright coals were burning in the fireplace, and all seemed light and warm within.

The little wanderer crept closer and closer to the window-pane. So sweet was the mother's face, so loving seemed the little children, that at last he took courage and tapped gently, very gently, on the door. The mother stopped talking, the little children looked up. "What was that, mother?" asked the little girl at her side. "I think it was some one tapping on the door," replied the mother. "Run as quickly as you can and open it, dear, for it is a bitter cold night to keep any one waiting in this storm."

"Oh, mother, I think it was the bough of the tree tapping against the window-pane," said the little girl. "Do please go on with our story." Again the little wanderer tapped upon the door.

"My child! my child," exclaimed the mother, rising, "that certainly was a rap on the door. Run quickly and open it. No one must be left out in the cold on our beautiful Christmas Eve."

The child ran to the door and threw it wide open. The mother saw the ragged stranger standing without, cold and shivering, with bare head and almost bare feet. She held out both hands and drew him into the warm, bright room. "You poor dear child," was all she said, and putting her arms around him, she drew him close to her breast. "He is very cold, my children," she exclaimed. "We must warm him."

"And," added the little girl, "we must love him and give him some of our Christmas, too."

75

"Yes," said the mother, "but first let us warm him."

The mother sat down beside the fire with the child on her lap, and her own two little ones warmed his half-frozen hands in theirs. The mother smoothed his tangled curls, and bending low over his head, kissed the child's face. She gathered the three little ones in her arms and the candle and the fire light shone over them. For a moment the room was very still. By and by the little girl said, softly, to her mother, "May we not light the Christmas tree, and let him see how beautiful it looks?"

"Yes," said the mother. With that she seated the child on a low stool beside the fire, and went herself to fetch the few simple ornaments which from year to year she had saved for her children's Christmas tree. They were soon so busy that they did not notice the room had filled with a strange and brilliant light. They turned and looked at the spot where the little wanderer sat. His ragged clothes had changed to garments white and beautiful; his tangled curls seemed like a halo of golden light about his head; but most glorious of all was his face, which shone with a light so dazzling that they could scarcely look upon it.

In silent wonder they gazed at the child. Their little room seemed to grow larger and larger until it was as wide as the whole world, the roof of their low house seemed to expand and rise, until it reached to the sky.

With a sweet and gentle smile the wonderful child looked upon them for a moment, and then slowly rose and floated through the air, above the treetops, beyond the church spire, higher even than the clouds themselves, until he appeared to them to be a shining star in the sky above. At last he disappeared from sight. The astonished children turned in hushed awe to their mother, and said, in a whisper, "Oh, mother, it was the Christ Child, was it not?" And the mother answered in a low tone, "Yes."

And it is said, dear children, that each Christmas Eve the little Christ Child wanders through some town or village, and those who receive him and take him into their homes and hearts have given to them this marvelous vision which is denied to others.

L. FRANK BAUM

1856-1919

THE LIFE AND ADVENTURES
OF SANTA CLAUS

Youth

1. Burzee

Have you heard of the great Forest of Burzee? Nurse used to sing of it when I was a child. She sang of the big tree trunks, standing close together, with their roots intertwining below the earth and their branches intertwining above it; of their rough coating of bark and queer, gnarled limbs; of the bushy foliage that roofed the entire forest, save where the sunbeams found a path through which to touch the ground in little spots and to cast weird and curious shadows over the mosses, the lichens and the drifts of dried leaves.

The Forest of Burzee is mighty and grand and awesome to those who steal beneath its shade. Coming from the sunlit meadows into its mazes it seems at first gloomy, then pleasant, and afterward filled with never-ending delights.

For hundreds of years it has flourished in all its magnificence, the silence of its enclosure unbroken save by the chirp of busy chipmunks, the growl of wild beasts and the songs of birds.

Yet Burzee has its inhabitants—for all this. Nature peopled it in the beginning with Fairies, Knooks, Ryls and Nymphs. As long as the Forest stands it will be a home, a refuge and a playground to these sweet immortals, who revel undisturbed in its depths.

Civilization has never yet reached Burzee. Will it ever, I wonder?

2. The Child of the Forest

Once, so long ago our great-grandfathers could scarcely have heard it mentioned, there lived within the great Forest of Burzee a wood-nymph named Necile. She was closely related to the mighty Queen Zurline, and her home was beneath the shade of a widespreading oak. Once every year, on Budding Day, when the trees put forth their new buds, Necile held the Golden Chalice of Ak to the lips of the Queen, who drank therefrom to the prosperity of the Forest. So you see she was a nymph of some importance, and, moreover, it is said she was highly regarded because of her beauty and grace.

When she was created she could not have told; Queen Zurline could not have told; the great Ak himself could not have told. It was long ago when the world was new and nymphs were needed to guard the forests and to minister to the wants of the young trees. Then, on some day not remembered, Necile sprang into being; radiant, lovely, straight and slim as the sapling she was created to guard.

Her hair was the color that lines a chestnut-bur; her eyes were blue in the sunlight and purple in the shade; her cheeks bloomed with the faint pink that edges the clouds at sunset; her lips were full red, pouting and sweet. For costume she adopted oak-leaf green; all the wood-nymphs dress in that color and know no other so desirable. Her dainty feet were sandal-clad, while her head remained bare of covering other than her silken tresses.

Necile's duties were few and simple. She kept hurtful weeds from growing beneath her trees and sapping the earth-food required by her charges. She frightened away the Gadgols, who took evil delight in flying against the tree trunks and wounding them so that they drooped and died from the poisonous contact. In dry seasons she carried water from the brooks and pools and moistened the roots of her thirsty dependents.

That was in the beginning. The weeds had now learned to avoid the forests where wood-nymphs dwelt; the loathsome Gadgols no longer dared come nigh; the trees had become old and sturdy and could bear the drought better than when fresh-sprouted. So Necile's duties were lessened, and time grew laggard, while succeeding years became more tiresome and uneventful than the nymph's joyous spirit loved.

Truly the forest-dwellers did not lack amusement. Each full moon they danced in the Royal Circle of the Queen. There were also the Feast of Nuts, the Jubilee of Autumn Tintings, the solemn ceremony of Leaf Shedding and the revelry of Budding Day. But these periods of enjoyment were far apart, and left many weary hours between.

That a wood-nymph should grow discontented was not thought of by Necile's sisters. It came upon her only after many years of brooding. But when once she had settled in her mind that life was irksome she had no patience with her condition, and longed to do something of real interest and to pass her days in ways hitherto undreamed of by forest nymphs. The Law of the Forest alone restrained her from going forth in search of adventure.

While this mood lay heavy upon pretty Necile it chanced that the great Ak visited the Forest of Burzee and allowed the wood-nymphs as was their wont—to lie at his feet and listen to the words of wisdom that fell from his lips. Ak is the Master Woodsman of the world; he sees everything, and knows more than the sons of men.

That night he held the Queen's hand, for he loved the nymphs as a father loves his children;

and Necile lay at his feet with many of her sisters and earnestly harkened as he spoke.

"We live so happily, my fair ones, in our forest glades," said Ak, stroking his grizzled beard thoughtfully, "that we know nothing of the sorrow and misery that fall to the lot of those poor mortals who inhabit the open spaces of the earth. They are not of our race, it is true, yet compassion well befits beings so fairly favored as ourselves. Often as I pass by the dwelling of some suffering mortal I am tempted to stop and banish the poor thing's misery. Yet suffering, in moderation, is the natural lot of mortals, and it is not our place to interfere with the laws of Nature."

"Nevertheless," said the fair Queen, nodding her golden head at the Master Woodsman, "it would not be a vain guess that Ak has often assisted these hapless mortals."

Ak smiled.

"Sometimes," he replied, "when they are very young—'children,' the mortals call them—I have stopped to rescue them from misery. The men and women I dare not interfere with; they must bear the burdens Nature has imposed upon them. But the helpless infants, the innocent children of men, have a right to be happy until they become full-grown and able to bear the trials of humanity. So I feel I am justified in assisting them. Not long ago—a year, maybe—I found four poor children huddled in a wooden hut, slowly freezing to death. Their parents had gone to a neighboring village for food, and had left a fire to warm their little ones while they were absent. But a storm arose and drifted the snow in their path, so they were long on the road. Meantime the fire went out and the frost crept into the bones of the waiting children."

"Poor things!" murmured the Queen softly. "What did you do?"

"I called Nelko, bidding him fetch wood from my forests and breathe upon it until the fire blazed again and warmed the little room where the children lay. Then they ceased shivering and fell asleep until their parents came."

"I am glad you did thus," said the good Queen, beaming upon the Master; and Necile, who had eagerly listened to every word, echoed in a whisper: "I, too, am glad!"

"And this very night," continued Ak, "as I came to the edge of Burzee I heard a feeble cry, which I judged came from a human infant. I looked about me and found, close to the forest, a helpless babe, lying quite naked upon the grasses and wailing piteously. Not far away, screened by the forest, crouched Shiegra, the lioness, intent upon devouring the infant for her evening meal."

"And what did you do, Ak?" asked the Queen, breathlessly.

"Not much, being in a hurry to greet my nymphs. But I commanded Shiegra to lie close to the babe, and to give it her milk to quiet its hunger. And I told her to send word throughout the forest, to all beasts and reptiles, that the child should not be harmed."

"I am glad you did thus," said the good Queen again, in a tone of relief; but this time Necile did not echo her words, for the nymph, filled with a strange resolve, had suddenly stolen away from the group.

Swiftly her lithe form darted through the forest paths until she reached the edge of mighty Burzee, when she paused to gaze curiously about her. Never until now had she ventured so far, for the Law of the Forest had placed the nymphs in its inmost depths.

Necile knew she was breaking the Law, but the thought did not give pause to her dainty feet. She had decided to see with her own eyes this infant Ak had told of, for she had never yet beheld a child of man. All the immortals are full-grown; there are no children among them. Peering through the trees Necile saw the child lying on the grass. But now it was sweetly sleeping, having been comforted by the milk drawn from Shiegra. It was not old enough to know what peril means; if it did not feel hunger it was content.

Softly the nymph stole to the side of the babe and knelt upon the sward, her long robe of rose leaf color spreading about her like a gossamer cloud. Her lovely countenance expressed curiosity and surprise, but, most of all, a tender, womanly pity. The babe was newborn, chubby and pink.

It was entirely helpless. While the nymph gazed the infant opened its eyes, smiled upon her, and stretched out two dimpled arms. In another instant Necile had caught it to her breast and was hurrying with it through the forest paths.

3. The Adoption

The Master Woodsman suddenly rose, with knitted brows. "There is a strange presence in the Forest," he declared. Then the Queen and her nymphs turned and saw standing before them Necile, with the sleeping infant clasped tightly in her arms and a defiant look in her deep blue eyes.

And thus for a moment they remained, the nymphs filled with surprise and consternation, but the brow of the Master Woodsman gradually clearing as he gazed intently upon the beautiful immortal who had willfully broken the Law. Then the great Ak, to the wonder of all, laid his hand softly on Necile's flowing locks and kissed her on her fair forehead.

"For the first time within my knowledge," said he, gently, "a nymph has defied me and my laws; yet in my heart can I find no word of chiding. What is your desire, Necile?"

"Let me keep the child!" she answered, beginning to tremble and falling on her knees in supplication.

"Here, in the Forest of Burzee, where the human race has never yet penetrated?" questioned Ak.

"Here, in the Forest of Burzee," replied the nymph, boldly. "It is my home, and I am weary for lack of occupation. Let me care for the babe! See how weak and helpless it is. Surely it cannot harm Burzee nor the Master Woodsman of the World!"

"But the Law, child, the Law!" cried Ak, sternly.

"The Law is made by the Master Woodsman," returned Necile; "if he bids me care for the babe he himself has saved from death, who in all the world dare oppose me?" Queen Zurline, who had listened intently to this conversation, clapped her pretty hands gleefully at the nymph's answer.

"You are fairly trapped, O Ak!" she exclaimed,

laughing. "Now, I pray you, give heed to Necile's petition."

The Woodsman, as was his habit when in thought, stroked his grizzled beard slowly. Then he said: "She shall keep the babe, and I will give it my protection. But I warn you all that as this is the first time I have relaxed the Law, so shall it be the last time. Never more, to the end of the World, shall a mortal be adopted by an immortal. Otherwise would we abandon our happy existence for one of trouble and anxiety. Good night, my nymphs!"

Then Ak was gone from their midst, and Necile hurried away to her bower to rejoice over her new-found treasure.

4. Claus

Another day found Necile's bower the most popular place in the Forest. The nymphs clustered around her and the child that lay asleep in her lap, with expressions of curiosity and delight. Nor were they wanting in praises for the great Ak's kindness in allowing Necile to keep the babe and to care for it. Even the Queen came to peer into the innocent childish face and to hold a helpless, chubby fist in her own fair hand.

"What shall we call him, Necile?" she asked, smiling. "He must have a name, you know."

"Let him be called Claus," answered Necile, "for that means 'a little one.'"

"Rather let him be called Neclaus,"[1] returned the Queen, "for that will mean 'Necile's little one.'"

The nymphs clapped their hands in delight, and Neclaus became the infant's name, although Necile loved best to call him Claus, and in after-days many of her sisters followed her example.

Necile gathered the softest moss in all the forest for Claus to lie upon, and she made his bed in her own bower. Of food the infant had no lack. The nymphs searched the forest for bell-udders, which grow upon the goa-tree and when opened are found to be filled with sweet milk. And the soft-eyed does willingly gave a share of their milk

---

1 Some people have spelled this name Nicklaus and others Nicolas, which is the reason that Santa Claus is still known in some lands as St. Nicolas. But, of course, Neclaus is his right name, and Claus the nickname given him by his adopted mother, the fair nymph Necile.

to support the little stranger, while Shiegra, the lioness, often crept stealthily into Necile's bower and purred softly as she lay beside the babe and fed it.

So the little one flourished and grew big and sturdy day by day, while Necile taught him to speak and to walk and to play.

His thoughts and words were sweet and gentle, for the nymphs knew no evil and their hearts were pure and loving. He became the pet of the forest, for Ak's decree had forbidden beast or reptile to molest him, and he walked fearlessly wherever his will guided him.

Presently the news reached the other immortals that the nymphs of Burzee had adopted a human infant, and that the act had been sanctioned by the great Ak. Therefore many of them came to visit the little stranger, looking upon him with much interest. First the Ryls, who are first cousins to the wood-nymphs, although so differently formed. For the Ryls are required to watch over the flowers and plants, as the nymphs watch over the forest trees. They search the wide world for the food required by the roots of the flowering plants, while the brilliant colors possessed by the full-blown flowers are due to the dyes placed in the soil by the Ryls, which are drawn through the little veins in the roots and the body of the plants, as they reach maturity. The Ryls are a busy people, for their flowers bloom and fade continually, but they are merry and light-hearted and are very popular with the other immortals.

Next came the Knooks, whose duty it is to watch over the beasts of the world, both gentle and wild. The Knooks have a hard time of it, since many of the beasts are ungovernable and rebel against restraint. But they know how to manage them, after all, and you will find that certain laws of the Knooks are obeyed by even the most ferocious animals. Their anxieties make the Knooks look old and worn and crooked, and their natures are a bit rough from associating with wild creatures continually; yet they are most useful to humanity and to the world in general, as their laws are the only laws the forest beasts recognize except those of the Master Woodsman.

Then there were the Fairies, the guardians of mankind, who were much interested in the adoption of Claus because their own laws forbade them to become familiar with their human charges. There are instances on record where the Fairies have shown themselves to human beings, and have even conversed with them; but they are supposed to guard the lives of mankind unseen and unknown, and if they favor some people more than others it is because these have won such distinction fairly, as the Fairies are very just and impartial. But the idea of adopting a child of men had never occurred to them because it was in every way opposed to their laws; so their curiosity was intense to behold the little stranger adopted by Necile and her sister nymphs.

Claus looked upon the immortals who thronged around him with fearless eyes and smiling lips. He rode laughingly upon the shoulders of the merry Ryls; he mischievously pulled the gray beards of the low-browed Knooks; he rested his curly head confidently upon the dainty bosom of the Fairy Queen herself. And the Ryls loved the

sound of his laughter; the Knooks loved his courage; the Fairies loved his innocence.

The boy made friends of them all, and learned
to know their laws intimately. No forest flower
was trampled beneath his feet, lest the friendly
Ryls should be grieved. He never interfered with
the beasts of the forest, lest his friends the Knooks
should become angry. The Fairies he loved dearly,
but, knowing nothing of mankind, he could not
understand that he was the only one of his race
admitted to friendly intercourse with them.

Indeed, Claus came to consider that he alone, of
all the forest people, had no like nor fellow. To him
the forest was the world. He had no idea that millions of toiling, striving human creatures existed.

And he was happy and content.

5. The Master Woodsman

Years pass swiftly in Burzee, for the nymphs
have no need to regard time in any way. Even
centuries make no change in the dainty creatures;
ever and ever they remain the same, immortal and
unchanging.

Claus, however, being mortal, grew to manhood day by day. Necile was disturbed, presently, to find him too big to lie in her lap, and he had a desire for other food than milk. His stout legs carried him far into Burzee's heart, where he gathered supplies of nuts and berries, as well as several sweet and wholesome roots, which suited his stomach better than the belludders. He sought Necile's bower less frequently, till finally it became his custom to return thither only to sleep.

The nymph, who had come to love him dearly, was puzzled to comprehend the changed nature of her charge, and unconsciously altered her own mode of life to conform to his whims. She followed him readily through the forest paths, as did many of her sister nymphs, explaining as they walked all the mysteries of the gigantic wood and the habits and nature of the living things which dwelt beneath its shade.

The language of the beasts became clear to little Claus; but he never could understand their sulky and morose tempers. Only the squirrels, the mice and the rabbits seemed to possess cheerful and merry natures; yet would the boy laugh when the panther growled, and stroke the bear's glossy coat while the creature snarled and bared its teeth menacingly. The growls and snarls were not for Claus, he well knew, so what did they matter?

He could sing the songs of the bees, recite the poetry of the wood-flowers and relate the history of every blinking owl in Burzee. He helped the Ryls to feed their plants and the Knooks to keep order among the animals. The little immortals regarded him as a privileged person, being especially protected by Queen Zurline and her nymphs and favored by the great Ak himself.

One day the Master Woodsman came back to the forest of Burzee. He had visited, in turn, all his forests throughout the world, and they were many and broad.

Not until he entered the glade where the Queen and her nymphs were assembled to greet him did Ak remember the child he had permitted Necile to adopt. Then he found, sitting familiarly in the circle of lovely immortals, a broad-shouldered, stalwart youth, who, when erect, stood fully as high as the shoulder of the Master himself.

Ak paused, silent and frowning, to bend his piercing gaze upon Claus. The clear eyes met his own steadfastly, and the Woodsman gave a sigh of relief as he marked their placid depths and read the youth's brave and innocent heart. Nevertheless, as Ak sat beside the fair Queen, and the golden chalice, filled with rare nectar, passed from lip to lip, the Master Woodsman was strangely silent and reserved, and stroked his beard many times with a thoughtful motion.

With morning he called Claus aside, in kindly fashion, saying: "Bid goodbye, for a time, to Necile and her sisters; for you shall accompany me on my journey through the world."

The venture pleased Claus, who knew well the honor of being companion of the Master Woodsman of the world. But Necile wept for the first time in her life, and clung to the boy's neck as if she could not bear to let him go. The nymph who had mothered this sturdy youth was still as dainty, as charming and beautiful as when she had dared to face Ak with the babe clasped to her breast; nor was her love less great. Ak beheld the two clinging together, seemingly as brother and sister to one another, and again he wore his thoughtful look.

6. Claus Discovers Humanity

Taking Claus to a small clearing in the forest, the Master said: "Place your hand upon my girdle and hold fast while we journey through the air; for now shall we encircle the world and look upon many of the haunts of those men from whom you are descended."

These words caused Claus to marvel, for until now he had thought himself the only one of his kind upon the earth; yet in silence he grasped firmly the girdle of the great Ak, his astonishment forbidding speech.

Then the vast forest of Burzee seemed to fall away from their feet, and the youth found himself passing swiftly through the air at a great height.

Ere long there were spires beneath them, while

buildings of many shapes and colors met their downward view. It was a city of men, and Ak, pausing to descend, led Claus to its enclosure. Said the Master: "So long as you hold fast to my girdle you will remain unseen by all mankind, though seeing clearly yourself. To release your grasp will be to separate yourself forever from me and your home in Burzee."

One of the first laws of the Forest is obedience, and Claus had no thought of disobeying the Master's wish. He clung fast to the girdle and remained invisible.

Thereafter with each moment passed in the city the youth's wonder grew. He, who had supposed himself created differently from all others, now found the earth swarming with creatures of his own kind.

"Indeed," said Ak, "the immortals are few; but the mortals are many."

Claus looked earnestly upon his fellows. There were sad faces, gay and reckless faces, pleasant faces, anxious faces and kindly faces, all mingled in puzzling disorder. Some worked at tedious tasks;

some strutted in impudent conceit; some were thoughtful and grave while others seemed happy and content. Men of many natures were there, as everywhere, and Claus found much to please him and much to make him sad.

But especially he noted the children—first curiously, then eagerly, then lovingly. Ragged little ones rolled in the dust of the streets, playing with scraps and pebbles. Other children, gaily dressed, were propped upon cushions and fed with sugar-plums. Yet the children of the rich were not happier than those playing with the dust and pebbles, it seemed to Claus.

"Childhood is the time of man's greatest content," said Ak, following the youth's thoughts. "'Tis during these years of innocent pleasure that the little ones are most free from care."

"Tell me," said Claus, "why do not all these babies fare alike?"

"Because they are born in both cottage and palace," returned the Master. "The difference in the wealth of the parents determines the lot of the child. Some are carefully tended and clothed in silks and dainty linen; others are neglected and covered with rags."

"Yet all seem equally fair and sweet," said Claus, thoughtfully.

"While they are babes—yes," agreed Ak. "Their joy is in being alive, and they do not stop to think. In after years the doom of mankind overtakes them, and they find they must struggle and worry, work and fret, to gain the wealth that is so dear to the hearts of men. Such things are unknown in the Forest where you were reared."

Claus was silent a moment. Then he asked: "Why was I reared in the forest, among those who are not of my race?"

Then Ak, in gentle voice, told him the story of his babyhood: how he had been abandoned at the forest's edge and left a prey to wild beasts, and how the loving nymph Necile had rescued him and brought him to manhood under the protection of the immortals.

"Yet I am not of them," said Claus, musingly.

"You are not of them," returned the Woodsman. "The nymph who cared for you as a mother seems now like a sister to you; by and by, when you grow old and gray, she will seem like a daughter. Yet another brief span and you will be but a memory, while she remains Necile."

"Then why, if man must perish, is he born?" demanded the boy.

"Everything perishes except the world itself and its keepers," answered Ak. "But while life lasts everything on earth has its use. The wise seek ways to be helpful to the world, for the helpful ones are sure to live again."

Much of this Claus failed to understand fully, but a longing seized him to become helpful to his fellows, and he remained grave and thoughtful while they resumed their journey.

They visited many dwellings of men in many parts of the world, watching farmers toil in the fields, warriors dash into cruel fray, and merchants exchange their goods for bits of white and yellow metal. And everywhere the eyes of Claus sought out the children in love and pity, for the thought of his own helpless babyhood was strong within him and he yearned to give help to the innocent little ones of his race even as he had been succored by the kindly nymph.

Day by day the Master Woodsman and his pupil traversed the earth, Ak speaking but seldom to the youth who clung steadfastly to his girdle, but guiding him into all places where he might become familiar with the lives of human beings.

And at last they returned to the grand old Forest of Burzee, where the Master set Claus down within the circle of nymphs, among whom the pretty Necile anxiously awaited him.

The brow of the great Ak was now calm and peaceful; but the brow of Claus had become lined with deep thought. Necile sighed at the change in her foster-son, who until now had been ever joyous and smiling, and the thought came to her that never again would the life of the boy be the same as before this eventful journey with the Master.

7. Claus Leaves the Forest

When good Queen Zurline had touched the golden chalice with her fair lips and it had passed around the circle in honor of the travelers' return, the Master Woodsman of the World, who had not yet spoken, turned his gaze frankly upon Claus and said: "Well?"

The boy understood, and rose slowly to his feet beside Necile. Once only his eyes passed around the familiar circle of nymphs, every one of whom he remembered as a loving comrade; but tears came unbidden to dim his sight, so he gazed thereafter steadfastly at the Master.

"I have been ignorant," said he, simply, "until the great Ak in his kindness taught me who and what I am. You, who live so sweetly in your forest bowers, ever fair and youthful and innocent, are no fit comrades for a son of humanity. For I have looked upon man, finding him doomed to live for a brief space upon earth, to toil for the things he needs, to fade into old age, and then to pass away as the leaves in autumn. Yet every man has his mission, which is to leave the world better, in some way, than he found it. I am of the race of men, and man's lot is my lot. For your tender care of the poor, forsaken babe you adopted, as well as for your loving comradeship during my boyhood, my heart will ever overflow with gratitude. My foster-mother," here he stopped and kissed Necile's white forehead, "I shall love and cherish while life lasts. But I must leave you, to take my part in the endless struggle to which humanity is doomed, and to live my life in my own way."

"What will you do?" asked the Queen, gravely.

"I must devote myself to the care of the children of mankind, and try to make them happy," he answered. "Since your own tender care of a babe brought to me happiness and strength, it is just and right that I devote my life to the pleasure of other babes. Thus will the memory of the loving nymph Necile be planted within the hearts of thousands of my race for many years to come, and her kindly act be recounted in song and in story while the world shall last. Have I spoken well, O Master?"

"You have spoken well," returned Ak, and rising to his feet he continued: "Yet one thing must not be forgotten. Having been adopted as the child of the Forest, and the playfellow of the nymphs, you have gained a distinction which forever separates you from your kind. Therefore, when you go forth into the world of men you shall retain the protection of the Forest, and the powers you now enjoy will remain with you to assist you in your labors. In any need you may call upon the Nymphs, the Ryls, the Knooks and the Fairies, and they will serve you gladly. I, the Master Woodsman of the World, have said it, and my Word is the Law!"

Claus looked upon Ak with grateful eyes.

"This will make me mighty among men," he replied. "Protected by these kind friends I may be able to make thousands of little children happy. I will try very hard to do my duty, and I know the Forest people will give me their sympathy and help."

"We will!" said the Fairy Queen, earnestly.

"We will!" cried the merry Ryls, laughing.

"We will!" shouted the crooked Knooks, scowling.

"We will!" exclaimed the sweet nymphs, proudly. But Necile said nothing. She only folded Claus in her arms and kissed him tenderly.

"The world is big," continued the boy, turning

again to his loyal friends, "but men are everywhere. I shall begin my work near my friends, so that if I meet with misfortune I can come to the Forest for counsel or help."

With that he gave them all a loving look and turned away. There was no need to say good by, by for him the sweet, wild life of the Forest was over. He went forth bravely to meet his doom—the doom of the race of man—the necessity to worry and work.

But Ak, who knew the boy's heart, was merciful and guided his steps.

.   .   .

Coming through Burzee to its eastern edge Claus reached the Laughing Valley of Hohaho. On each side were rolling green hills, and a brook wandered midway between them to wind afar off beyond the valley. At his back was the grim Forest; at the far end of the valley a broad plain. The eyes of the young man, which had until now reflected his grave thoughts, became brighter as he stood silent, looking out upon the Laughing Valley. Then on a sudden his eyes twinkled, as stars do on a still night, and grew merry and wide.

For at his feet the cowslips and daisies smiled on him in friendly regard; the breeze whistled gaily as it passed by and fluttered the locks on his forehead; the brook laughed joyously as it leaped over the pebbles and swept around the green curves of its banks; the bees sang sweet songs as they flew from dandelion to daffodil; the beetles chirruped happily in the long grass, and the sunbeams glinted pleasantly over all the scene.

"Here," cried Claus, stretching out his arms as if to embrace the Valley, "will I make my home!"

That was many, many years ago. It has been his home ever since. It is his home now.

Manhood

1. The Laughing Valley

When Claus came the Valley was empty save for the grass, the brook, the wildflowers, the bees and the butterflies. If he would make his home here and live after the fashion of men he must have a house. This puzzled him at first, but while he stood smiling in the sunshine he suddenly found beside him old Nelko, the servant of the Master Woodsman. Nelko bore an ax, strong and broad, with a blade that gleamed like burnished silver. This he placed in the young man's hand, then disappeared without a word.

Claus understood, and turning to the Forest's edge he selected a number of fallen tree trunks, which he began to clear of their dead branches. He would not cut into a living tree. His life among the nymphs who guarded the Forest had taught him that a live tree is sacred, being a created thing endowed with feeling. But with the dead and fallen trees it was different. They had fulfilled their destiny, as active members of the Forest community, and now it was fitting that their remains should minister to the needs of man.

The ax bit deep into the logs at every stroke. It seemed to have a force of its own, and Claus had but to swing and guide it.

When shadows began creeping over the green hills to lie in the Valley overnight, the young man had chopped many logs into equal lengths and proper shapes for building a house such as he had seen the poorer classes of men inhabit. Then, resolving to await another day before he tried to fit the logs together, Claus ate some of the sweet roots he well knew how to find, drank deeply from the laughing brook, and lay down to sleep on the grass, first seeking a spot where no flowers grew, lest the weight of his body should crush them.

And while he slumbered and breathed in the perfume of the wondrous Valley the Spirit of Happiness crept into his heart and drove out all terror and care and misgivings. Never more would the face of Claus be clouded with anxieties; never more would the trials of life weigh him down as with a burden. The Laughing Valley had claimed him for its own.

Would that we all might live in that delightful place!—but then, maybe, it would become overcrowded. For ages it had awaited a tenant.

Was it chance that led young Claus to make his home in this happy vale? Or may we guess that his thoughtful friends, the immortals, had directed his steps when he wandered away from Burzee to seek a home in the great world?

Certain it is that while the moon peered over the hilltop and flooded with its soft beams the body of the sleeping stranger, the Laughing Valley was filled with the queer, crooked shapes of the friendly Knooks. These people spoke no words, but worked with skill and swiftness. The logs Claus had trimmed with his bright ax were carried to a spot beside the brook and fitted one upon another, and during the night a strong and roomy dwelling was built.

The birds came sweeping into the Valley at daybreak, and their songs, so seldom heard in the deep wood, aroused the stranger. He rubbed the web of sleep from his eyelids and looked around. The house met his gaze.

"I must thank the Knooks for this," said he, gratefully. Then he walked to his dwelling and entered at the doorway. A large room faced him, having a fireplace at the end and a table and bench in the middle. Beside the fireplace was a cupboard. Another doorway was beyond. Claus entered here, also, and saw a smaller room with a bed against the wall and a stool set near a small stand. On the bed were many layers of dried moss brought from the Forest.

"Indeed, it is a palace!" exclaimed the smiling Claus. "I must thank the good Knooks again, for their knowledge of man's needs as well as for their labors in my behalf."

He left his new home with a glad feeling that he was not quite alone in the world, although he had chosen to abandon his Forest life. Friendships are not easily broken, and the immortals are everywhere.

Upon reaching the brook he drank of the pure water, and then sat down on the bank to laugh at the mischievous gambols of the ripples as they pushed one another against rocks or crowded desperately to see which should first reach the turn beyond. And as they raced away he listened to the song they sang:

"Rushing, pushing, on we go!
Not a wave may gently flow—
All are too excited.
Ev'ry drop, delighted,
Turns to spray in merry play
As we tumble on our way!"

Next Claus searched for roots to eat, while the daffodils turned their little eyes up to him laughingly and lisped their dainty song:

"Blooming fairly, growing rarely,
Never flowerets were so gay!
Perfume breathing, joy bequeathing,
As our colors we display."

It made Claus laugh to hear the little things voice their happiness as they nodded gracefully on their stems. But another strain caught his ear as the sunbeams fell gently across his face and whispered:

"Here is gladness, that our rays
Warm the valley through the days;

Here is happiness, to give
Comfort unto all who live!"

"Yes!" cried Claus in answer, "there is happiness and joy in all things here. The Laughing Valley is a valley of peace and good-will."

He passed the day talking with the ants and beetles and exchanging jokes with the light-hearted butterflies. And at night he lay on his bed of soft moss and slept soundly.

Then came the Fairies, merry but noiseless, bringing skillets and pots and dishes and pans and all the tools necessary to prepare food and to comfort a mortal. With these they filled cupboard and fireplace, finally placing a stout suit of wool clothing on the stool by the bedside.

When Claus awoke he rubbed his eyes again, and laughed, and spoke aloud his thanks to the Fairies and the Master Woodsman who had sent them. With eager joy he examined all his new possessions, wondering what some might be used for. But, in the days when he had clung to the girdle of the great Ak and visited the cities of men, his eyes had been quick to note all the manners and customs of the race to which he belonged; so he guessed from the gifts brought by the Fairies that the Master expected him hereafter to live in the fashion of his fellow-creatures.

"Which means that I must plow the earth and plant corn," he reflected; "so that when winter comes I shall have garnered food in plenty."

But, as he stood in the grassy Valley, he saw that to turn up the earth in furrows would be to destroy hundreds of pretty, helpless flowers, as well as thousands of the tender blades of grass. And this he could not bear to do.

Therefore he stretched out his arms and uttered a peculiar whistle he had learned in the Forest, afterward crying: "Ryls of the Field Flowers—come to me!"

Instantly a dozen of the queer little Ryls were squatting upon the ground before him, and they nodded to him in cheerful greeting.

Claus gazed upon them earnestly.

"Your brothers of the Forest," he said, "I have known and loved many years. I shall love you, also, when we have become friends. To me the laws of the Ryls, whether those of the Forest or of the field, are sacred. I have never willfully destroyed one of the flowers you tend so carefully; but I must plant grain to use for food during the cold winter, and how am I to do this without killing the little creatures that sing to me so prettily of their fragrant blossoms?"

The Yellow Ryl, he who tends the buttercups, made answer: "Fret not, friend Claus. The great Ak has spoken to us of you. There is better work for you in life than to labor for food, and though, not being of the Forest, Ak has no command over us, nevertheless are we glad to favor one he loves. Live, therefore, to do the good work you are resolved to undertake. We, the Field Ryls, will attend to your food supplies."

After this speech the Ryls were no longer to be seen, and Claus drove from his mind the thought of tilling the earth.

When next he wandered back to his dwelling a bowl of fresh milk stood upon the table; bread was in the cupboard and sweet honey filled a dish beside it. A pretty basket of rosy apples and new-plucked grapes was also awaiting him. He called out "Thanks, my friends!" to the invisible Ryls, and straightway began to eat of the food.

Thereafter, when hungry, he had but to look into the cupboard to find goodly supplies brought by the kindly Ryls. And the Knooks cut and stacked much wood for his fireplace. And the Fairies brought him warm blankets and clothing.

So began his life in the Laughing Valley, with the favor and friendship of the immortals to minister to his every want.

2. How Claus Made the First Toy

Truly our Claus had wisdom, for his good fortune but strengthened his resolve to befriend the little ones of his own race. He knew his plan was approved by the immortals, else they would not have favored him so greatly.

So he began at once to make acquaintance with mankind. He walked through the Valley to the plain beyond, and crossed the plain in many directions to reach the abodes of men. These stood singly or in groups of dwellings called villages, and in nearly all the houses, whether big or little, Claus found children.

The youngsters soon came to know his merry, laughing face and the kind glance of his bright eyes; and the parents, while they regarded the young man with some scorn for loving children more than their elders, were content that the girls and boys had found a playfellow who seemed willing to amuse them.

So the children romped and played games with Claus, and the boys rode upon his shoulders, and the girls nestled in his strong arms, and the babies clung fondly to his knees. Wherever the young man chanced to be, the sound of childish laughter followed him; and to understand this better you must know that children were much neglected in those days and received little attention from their parents, so that it became to them a marvel that so goodly a man as Claus devoted his time to making them happy. And those who knew him were, you may be sure, very happy indeed. The sad faces of the poor and abused grew bright for once; the cripple smiled despite his misfortune; the ailing ones hushed their moans and the grieved ones their cries when their merry friend came nigh to comfort them.

Only at the beautiful palace of the Lord of Lerd and at the frowning castle of the Baron Braun was Claus refused admittance. There were children at both places; but the servants at the palace shut the door in the young stranger's face, and the fierce Baron threatened to hang him from an iron hook on the castle walls. Whereupon Claus sighed and went back to the poorer dwellings where he was welcome.

After a time the winter drew near.

The flowers lived out their lives and faded and disappeared; the beetles burrowed far into the warm earth; the butterflies deserted the meadows; and the voice of the brook grew hoarse, as if it had taken cold.

One day snowflakes filled all the air in the Laughing Valley, dancing boisterously toward the earth and clothing in pure white raiment the roof of Claus's dwelling.

At night Jack Frost rapped at the door.

"Come in!" cried Claus.

"Come out!" answered Jack. "For you have a fire inside."

So Claus came out. He had known Jack Frost in the Forest, and liked the jolly rogue, even while he mistrusted him.

"There will be rare sport for me to-night, Claus!" shouted the sprite. "Isn't this glorious weather? I shall nip scores of noses and ears and toes before daybreak."

"If you love me, Jack, spare the children," begged Claus.

"And why?" asked the other, in surprise.

"They are tender and helpless," answered Claus.

"But I love to nip the tender ones!" declared Jack. "The older ones are tough, and tire my fingers."

"The young ones are weak, and cannot fight you," said Claus.

"True," agreed Jack, thoughtfully. "Well, I will not pinch a child this night—if I can resist the temptation," he promised. "Good night, Claus!"

"Good night."

The young man went in and closed the door, and Jack Frost ran on to the nearest village.

Claus threw a log on the fire, which burned up brightly. Beside the hearth sat Blinkie, a big cat give him by Peter the Knook. Her fur was soft and glossy, and she purred never-ending songs of contentment.

"I shall not see the children again soon," said Claus to the cat, who kindly paused in her song to listen. "The winter is upon us, the snow will be deep for many days, and I shall be unable to play with my little friends."

The cat raised a paw and stroked her nose thoughtfully, but made no reply. So long as the fire burned and Claus sat in his easy chair by the hearth she did not mind the weather.

So passed many days and many long evenings. The cupboard was always full, but Claus became weary with having nothing to do more than to feed the fire from the big wood-pile the Knooks had brought him.

One evening he picked up a stick of wood and began to cut it with his sharp knife. He had no thought, at first, except to occupy his time, and he whistled and sang to the cat as he carved away portions of the stick. Puss sat up on her haunches and watched him, listening at the same time to her master's merry whistle, which she loved to hear even more than her own purring songs.

Claus glanced at puss and then at the stick he was whittling, until presently the wood began to have a shape, and the shape was like the head of a cat, with two ears sticking upward.

Claus stopped whistling to laugh, and then both he and the cat looked at the wooden image in some surprise. Then he carved out the eyes and the nose, and rounded the lower part of the head so that it rested upon a neck.

Puss hardly knew what to make of it now, and sat up stiffly, as if watching with some suspicion what would come next.

Claus knew. The head gave him an idea. He plied his knife carefully and with skill, forming slowly the body of the cat, which he made to sit upon its haunches as the real cat did, with her tail wound around her two front legs.

The work cost him much time, but the evening was long and he had nothing better to do. Finally he gave a loud and delighted laugh at the result of his labors and placed the wooden cat, now completed, upon the hearth opposite the real one.

Puss thereupon glared at her image, raised her hair in anger, and uttered a defiant mew. The wooden cat paid no attention, and Claus, much amused, laughed again.

Then Blinkie advanced toward the wooden image to eye it closely and smell of it intelligently: Eyes and nose told her the creature was wood, in spite of its natural appearance; so puss resumed her seat and her purring, but as she neatly washed her face with her padded paw she cast more than one admiring glance at her clever master. Perhaps she felt the same satisfaction we feel when we look upon good photographs of ourselves.

The cat's master was himself pleased with his handiwork, without knowing exactly why.

Indeed, he had great cause to congratulate himself that night, and all the children throughout the world should have joined him rejoicing. For Claus had made his first toy.

3. How the Ryls Colored the Toys

A hush lay on the Laughing Valley now. Snow covered it like a white spread and pillows of downy flakes drifted before the dwelling where Claus sat feeding the blaze of the fire. The brook gurgled on beneath a heavy sheet of ice and all living plants and insects nestled close to Mother Earth to keep warm. The face of the moon was hid by dark clouds, and the wind, delighting in the wintry sport, pushed and whirled the snowflakes in so many directions that they could get no chance to fall to the ground.

Claus heard the wind whistling and shrieking in its play and thanked the good Knooks again for his comfortable shelter. Blinkie washed her face lazily and stared at the coals with a look of perfect content. The toy cat sat opposite the real one and gazed straight ahead, as toy cats should.

Suddenly Claus heard a noise that sounded different from the voice of the wind. It was more like a wail of suffering and despair.

He stood up and listened, but the wind, growing boisterous, shook the door and rattled the windows to distract his attention. He waited until the wind was tired and then, still listening, he heard once more the shrill cry of distress.

Quickly he drew on his coat, pulled his cap over his eyes and opened the door. The wind dashed in and scattered the embers over the hearth, at the same time blowing Blinkie's fur so furiously that she crept under the table to escape. Then the door was closed and Claus was outside, peering anxiously into the darkness.

The wind laughed and scolded and tried to push him over, but he stood firm. The helpless flakes stumbled against his eyes and dimmed his sight, but he rubbed them away and looked again. Snow was everywhere, white and glittering. It covered the earth and filled the air.

The cry was not repeated.

Claus turned to go back into the house, but the

wind caught him unawares and he stumbled and fell across a snowdrift. His hand plunged into the drift and touched something that was not snow. This he seized and, pulling it gently toward him, found it to be a child. The next moment he had lifted it in his arms and carried it into the house.

The wind followed him through the door, but Claus shut it out quickly. He laid the rescued child on the hearth, and brushing away the snow he discovered it to be Weekum, a little boy who lived in a house beyond the Valley.

Claus wrapped a warm blanket around the little one and rubbed the frost from its limbs. Before long the child opened his eyes and, seeing where he was, smiled happily. Then Claus warmed milk and fed it to the boy slowly, while the cat looked on with sober curiosity. Finally the little one curled up in his friend's arms and sighed and fell asleep, and Claus, filled with gladness that he had found the wanderer, held him closely while he slumbered.

The wind, finding no more mischief to do, climbed the hill and swept on toward the north.

This gave the weary snowflakes time to settle down to earth, and the Valley became still again.

The boy, having slept well in the arms of his friend, opened his eyes and sat up. Then, as a child will, he looked around the room and saw all that it contained.

"Your cat is a nice cat, Claus," he said, at last. "Let me hold it."

But puss objected and ran away.

"The other cat won't run, Claus," continued the boy. "Let me hold that one." Claus placed the toy in his arms, and the boy held it lovingly and kissed the tip of its wooden ear.

"How did you get lost in the storm, Weekum?" asked Claus.

"I started to walk to my auntie's house and lost my way," answered Weekum.

"Were you frightened?"

"It was cold," said Weekum, "and the snow got in my eyes, so I could not see. Then I kept on till I fell in the snow, without knowing where I was, and the wind blew the flakes over me and covered me up."

Claus gently stroked his head, and the boy looked up at him and smiled.

"I'm all right now," said Weekum.

"Yes," replied Claus, happily. "Now I will put you in my warm bed, and you must sleep until morning, when I will carry you back to your mother."

"May the cat sleep with me?" asked the boy.

"Yes, if you wish it to," answered Claus.

"It's a nice cat!" Weekum said, smiling, as Claus tucked the blankets around him; and presently the little one fell asleep with the wooden toy in his arms.

When morning came the sun claimed the Laughing Valley and flooded it with his rays; so Claus prepared to take the lost child back to its mother.

"May I keep the cat, Claus?" asked Weekum. "It's nicer than real cats. It doesn't run away, or scratch or bite. May I keep it?"

"Yes, indeed," answered Claus, pleased that the toy he had made could give pleasure to the child. So he wrapped the boy and the wooden cat in a warm cloak, perching the bundle upon his own broad shoulders, and then he tramped through the snow and the drifts of the Valley and across the plain beyond to the poor cottage where Weekum's mother lived.

"See, mama!" cried the boy, as soon as they entered. "I've got a cat!"

The good woman wept tears of joy over the rescue of her darling and thanked Claus many times for his kind act. So he carried a warm and happy heart back to his home in the Valley.

That night he said to puss: "I believe the children will love the wooden cats almost as well as the real ones, and they can't hurt them by pulling their tails and ears. I'll make another."

So this was the beginning of his great work.

The next cat was better made than the first. While Claus sat whittling it out the Yellow Ryl came in to make him a visit, and so pleased was he with the man's skill that he ran away and brought several of his fellows.

There sat the Red Ryl, the Black Ryl, the Green Ryl, the Blue Ryl and the Yellow Ryl in a circle on the floor, while Claus whittled and whistled and the wooden cat grew into shape.

"If it could be made the same color as the real cat, no one would know the difference," said the Yellow Ryl, thoughtfully.

"The little ones, maybe, would not know the difference," replied Claus, pleased with the idea.

"I will bring you some of the red that I color my roses and tulips with," cried the Red Ryl, "and then you can make the cat's lips and tongue red."

"I will bring some of the green that I color my grasses and leaves with," said the Green Ryl, "and then you can color the cat's eyes green."

"They will need a bit of yellow, also," remarked the Yellow Ryl. "I must fetch some of the yellow that I use to color my buttercups and goldenrods with."

"The real cat is black," said the Black Ryl. "I will bring some of the black that I use to color the eyes of my pansies with, and then you can paint your wooden cat black."

"I see you have a blue ribbon around Blinkie's neck," added the Blue Ryl. "I will get some of the color that I use to paint the bluebells and forget-me-nots with, and then you can carve a wooden ribbon on the toy cat's neck and paint it blue."

So the Ryls disappeared, and by the time Claus had finished carving out the form of the cat they were all back with the paints and brushes.

They made Blinkie sit upon the table, that Claus might paint the toy cat just the right color, and when the work was done the Ryls declared it was exactly as good as a live cat.

"That is, to all appearances," added the Red Ryl.

Blinkie seemed a little offended by the attention bestowed upon the toy, and that she might not seem to approve the imitation cat she walked to the corner of the hearth and sat down with a dignified air.

But Claus was delighted, and as soon as morning came he started out and tramped through the snow, across the Valley and the plain, until he came to a village. There, in a poor hut near the walls of the beautiful palace of the Lord of Lerd, a little girl lay upon a wretched cot, moaning with pain.

Claus approached the child and kissed her and comforted her, and then he drew the toy cat from beneath his coat, where he had hidden it, and placed it in her arms.

Ah, how well he felt himself repaid for his labor and his long walk when he saw the little one's eyes grow bright with pleasure! She hugged the kitty tight to her breast, as if it had been a precious gem, and would not let it go for a single moment. The fever was quieted, the pain grew less, and she fell into a sweet and refreshing sleep.

Claus laughed and whistled and sang all the way home. Never had he been so happy as on that day.

When he entered his house he found Shiegra, the lioness, awaiting him. Since his babyhood Shiegra had loved Claus, and while he dwelt in the Forest she had often come to visit him at Necile's bower. After Claus had gone to live in the Laughing Valley Shiegra became lonely and ill at ease, and now she had braved the snow-drifts, which all lions abhor, to see him once more. Shiegra was getting old and her teeth were beginning to fall out, while the hairs that tipped her ears and tail had changed from tawny-yellow to white.

Claus found her lying on his hearth, and he put his arms around the neck of the lioness and hugged her lovingly. The cat had retired into a far corner. She did not care to associate with Shiegra.

Claus told his old friend about the cats he had made, and how much pleasure they had given Weekum and the sick girl. Shiegra did not know much about children; indeed, if she met a child she could scarcely be trusted not to devour it. But she was interested in Claus's new labors, and said: "These images seem to me very attractive. Yet I cannot see why you should make cats, which are very unimportant animals. Suppose, now that I am here, you make the image of a lioness, the Queen of all beasts. Then, indeed, your children will be happy—and safe at the same time!"

Claus thought this was a good suggestion. So he got a piece of wood and sharpened his knife, while Shiegra crouched upon the hearth at his feet. With much care he carved the head in the likeness of the lioness, even to the two fierce teeth that curved over her lower lip and the deep, frowning lines above her wide-open eyes.

When it was finished he said: "You have a terrible look, Shiegra."

"Then the image is like me," she answered, "for I am indeed terrible to all who are not my friends."

Claus now carved out the body, with Shiegra's long tail trailing behind it. The image of the crouching lioness was very lifelike.

"It pleases me," said Shiegra, yawning and stretching her body gracefully. "Now I will watch while you paint."

He brought the paints the Ryls had given him from the cupboard and colored the image to resemble the real Shiegra.

The lioness placed her big, padded paws upon the edge of the table and raised herself while she carefully examined the toy that was her likeness.

"You are indeed skillful!" she said, proudly. "The children will like that better than cats, I'm sure."

Then snarling at Blinkie, who arched her back

in terror and whined fearfully, she walked away toward her forest home with stately strides.

4. How Little Mayrie Became Frightened

The winter was over now, and all the Laughing Valley was filled with joyous excitement. The brook was so happy at being free once again that it gurgled more boisterously than ever and dashed so recklessly against the rocks that it sent showers of spray high in the air. The grass thrust its sharp little blades upward through the mat of dead stalks where it had hidden from the snow, but the flowers were yet too timid to show themselves, although the Ryls were busy feeding their roots. The sun was in remarkably good humor, and sent his rays dancing merrily throughout the Valley.

Claus was eating his dinner one day when he heard a timid knock on his door.

"Come in!" he called.

No one entered, but after a pause came another rapping.

Claus jumped up and threw open the door.

Before him stood a small girl holding a smaller brother fast by the hand.

"Is you Tlaus?" she asked, shyly.

"Indeed I am, my dear!" he answered, with a laugh, as he caught both children in his arms and kissed them. "You are very welcome, and you have come just in time to share my dinner."

He took them to the table and fed them with fresh milk and nut-cakes. When they had eaten enough he asked: "Why have you made this long journey to see me?"

"I wants a tat!" replied little Mayrie; and her brother, who had not yet learned to speak many words, nodded his head and exclaimed like an echo: "Tat!"

"Oh, you want my toy cats, do you?" returned Claus, greatly pleased to discover that his creations were so popular with children.

The little visitors nodded eagerly.

"Unfortunately," he continued, "I have but one cat now ready, for I carried two to children in the town yesterday. And the one I have shall be given to your brother, Mayrie, because he is the smaller; and the next one I make shall be for you."

The boy's face was bright with smiles as he took the precious toy Claus held out to him; but little Mayrie covered her face with her arm and began to sob grievously.

"I—I—I wants a t—t—tat now!" she wailed.

Her disappointment made Claus feel miserable for a moment. Then he suddenly remembered Shiegra.

"Don't cry, darling!" he said, soothingly. "I have a toy much nicer than a cat, and you shall have that."

He went to the cupboard and drew out the image of the lioness, which he placed on the table before Mayrie.

The girl raised her arm and gave one glance at the fierce teeth and glaring eyes of the beast, and then, uttering a terrified scream, she rushed from the house. The boy followed her, also screaming lustily, and even dropping his precious cat in his fear.

For a moment Claus stood motionless, being

puzzled and astonished. Then he threw Shiegra's image into the cupboard and ran after the children, calling to them not to be frightened.

Little Mayrie stopped in her flight and her brother clung to her skirt; but they both cast fearful glances at the house until Claus had assured them many times that the beast had been locked in the cupboard.

"Yet why were you frightened at seeing it?" he asked. "It is only a toy to play with!"

"It's bad!" said Mayrie, decidedly, "an'—an'—just horrid, an' not a bit nice, like tats!"

"Perhaps you are right," returned Claus, thoughtfully. "But if you will return with me to the house I will soon make you a pretty cat."

So they timidly entered the house again, having faith in their friend's words; and afterward they had the joy of watching Claus carve out a cat from a bit of wood and paint it in natural colors. It did not take him long to do this, for he had become skillful with his knife by this time, and Mayrie loved her toy the more dearly because she had seen it made.

After his little visitors had trotted away on their journey homeward Claus sat long in deep thought. And he then decided that such fierce creatures as his friend the lioness would never do as models from which to fashion his toys.

"There must be nothing to frighten the dear babies," he reflected, "and while I know Shiegra well, and am not afraid of her, it is but natural that children should look upon her image with terror. Hereafter I will choose such mild-mannered animals as squirrels and rabbits and deer and lambkins from which to carve my toys, for then the little ones will love rather than fear them."

He began his work that very day, and before bedtime had made a wooden rabbit and a lamb. They were not quite so lifelike as the cats had been, because they were formed from memory, while Blinkie had sat very still for Claus to look at while he worked.

But the new toys pleased the children nevertheless, and the fame of Claus' playthings quickly spread to every cottage on plain and in village.

He always carried his gifts to the sick or crippled children, but those who were strong enough walked to the house in the Valley to ask for them, so a little path was soon worn from the plain to the door of the toy-maker's cottage.

First came the children who had been play-mates of Claus, before he began to make toys. These, you may be sure, were well supplied. Then children who lived farther away heard of the wonderful images and made journeys to the Valley to secure them. All little ones were welcome, and never a one went away empty-handed.

This demand for his handiwork kept Claus busily occupied, but he was quite happy in know-ing the pleasure he gave to so many of the dear children. His friends the immortals were pleased with his success and supported him bravely.

The Knooks selected for him clear pieces of soft wood, that his knife might not be blunted in cutting them; the Ryls kept him supplied with paints of all colors and brushes fashioned from the tips of timothy grasses; the Fairies discovered that the workman needed saws and chisels and hammers and nails, as well as knives, and brought him a goodly array of such tools.

Claus soon turned his living room into a most wonderful workshop. He built a bench before the window, and arranged his tools and paints so that he could reach everything as he sat on his stool. And as he finished toy after toy to delight the hearts of little children he found himself growing so gay and happy that he could not refrain from singing and laughing and whistling all the day long.

"It's because I live in the Laughing Valley, where everything else laughs!" said Claus.

But that was not the reason.

5. How Bessie Blithesome Came to the Laughing Valley

One day, as Claus sat before his door to enjoy the sunshine while he busily carved the head and horns of a toy deer, he looked up and discovered a glittering cavalcade of horsemen approaching through the Valley.

When they drew nearer he saw that the band consisted of a score of men-at-arms, clad in bright armor and bearing in their hands spears and battle-axes. In front of these rode little Bessie Blithesome, the pretty daughter of that proud Lord of Lerd who had once driven Claus from his palace. Her palfrey was pure white, its bridle was covered with glittering gems, and its saddle draped with cloth of gold, richly broidered. The soldiers were sent to protect her from harm while she journeyed.

Claus was surprised, but he continued to whittle and to sing until the cavalcade drew up before him. Then the little girl leaned over the neck of her palfrey and said: "Please, Mr. Claus, I want a toy!"

Her voice was so pleading that Claus jumped up at once and stood beside her. But he was puzzled how to answer her request.

"You are a rich lord's daughter," said he, "and have all that you desire."

"Except toys," added Bessie. "There are no toys in all the world but yours."

"And I make them for the poor children, who have nothing else to amuse them," continued Claus.

"Do poor children love to play with toys more than rich ones?" asked Bessie.

"I suppose not," said Claus, thoughtfully.

"Am I to blame because my father is a lord? Must I be denied the pretty toys I long for because other children are poorer than I?" she inquired earnestly.

"I'm afraid you must, dear," he answered, "for the poor have nothing else with which to amuse themselves. You have your pony to ride, your servants to wait on you, and every comfort that money can procure."

"But I want toys!" cried Bessie, wiping away the tears that forced themselves into her eyes. "If I cannot have them, I shall be very unhappy."

Claus was troubled, for her grief recalled to him the thought that his desire was to make all children happy, without regard to their condition in life. Yet, while so many poor children were clamoring for his toys he could not bear to give one of them to Bessie Blithesome, who had so much already to make her happy.

"Listen, my child," said he, gently, "all the toys I am now making are promised to others. But the next shall be yours, since your heart so longs for it. Come to me again in two days and it shall be ready for you."

Bessie gave a cry of delight, and leaning over her pony's neck she kissed Claus prettily upon his forehead. Then, calling to her men-at-arms, she rode gaily away, leaving Claus to resume his work.

"If I am to supply the rich children as well as the poor ones," he thought, "I shall not have a spare moment in the whole year! But is it right I should give to the rich? Surely I must go to Necile and talk with her about this matter."

So when he had finished the toy deer, which was very like a deer he had known in the Forest glades, he walked into Burzee and made his way to the bower of the beautiful Nymph Necile, who had been his foster mother.

She greeted him tenderly and lovingly, listening with interest to his story of the visit of Bessie Blithesome.

"And now tell me," said he, "shall I give toys to rich children?"

"We of the Forest know nothing of riches," she replied. "It seems to me that one child is like another child, since they are all made of the same clay, and that riches are like a gown, which may be put on or taken away, leaving the child unchanged. But the Fairies are guardians of mankind, and know mortal children better than I. Let us call the Fairy Queen."

This was done, and the Queen of the Fairies sat beside them and heard Claus relate his reasons for thinking the rich children could get along without his toys, and also what the Nymph had said.

"Necile is right," declared the Queen; "for, whether it be rich or poor, a child's longings for pretty playthings are but natural. Rich Bessie's heart may suffer as much grief as poor Mayrie's; she can be just as lonely and discontented, and just as gay and happy. I think, friend Claus, it is your duty to make all little ones glad, whether they chance to live in palaces or in cottages."

"Your words are wise, fair Queen," replied Claus, "and my heart tells me they are as just as they are wise. Hereafter all children may claim my services."

Then he bowed before the gracious Fairy and, kissing Necile's red lips, went back into his Valley.

At the brook he stopped to drink, and afterward he sat on the bank and took a piece of moist clay in his hands while he thought what sort of toy he should make for Bessie Blithesome. He did not notice that his fingers were working the clay into shape until, glancing downward, he found he had unconsciously formed a head that bore a slight resemblance to the Nymph Necile!

At once he became interested. Gathering more of the clay from the bank he carried it to his house. Then, with the aid of his knife and a bit of wood he succeeded in working the clay into the image of a toy nymph. With skillful strokes he formed long, waving hair on the head and covered the body with a gown of oakleaves, while the two feet sticking out at the bottom of the gown were clad in sandals.

But the clay was soft, and Claus found he must handle it gently to avoid ruining his pretty work.

"Perhaps the rays of the sun will draw out the moisture and cause the clay to become hard," he thought. So he laid the image on a flat board and placed it in the glare of the sun.

This done, he went to his bench and began painting the toy deer, and soon he became so interested in the work that he forgot all about the clay nymph. But next morning, happening to notice it as it lay on the board, he found the sun had baked it to the hardness of stone, and it was strong enough to be safely handled.

Claus now painted the nymph with great care in the likeness of Necile, giving it deep-blue eyes, white teeth, rosy lips and ruddy-brown hair. The gown he colored oak-leaf green, and when the paint was dry Claus himself was charmed with the new toy. Of course it was not nearly so lovely as the real Necile; but, considering the material of which it was made, Claus thought it was very beautiful.

When Bessie, riding upon her white palfrey, came to his dwelling next day, Claus presented her with the new toy. The little girl's eyes were brighter than ever as she examined the pretty image, and she loved it at once, and held it close to her breast, as a mother does to her child.

"What is it called, Claus?" she asked.

Now Claus knew that Nymphs do not like to be spoken of by mortals, so he could not tell Bessie it was an image of Necile he had given her. But as it was a new toy he searched his mind for a new name to call it by, and the first word he thought of he decided would do very well.

"It is called a dolly, my dear," he said to Bessie.

"I shall call the dolly my baby," returned Bessie, kissing it fondly; "and I shall tend it and care for it just as Nurse cares for me. Thank you very much, Claus; your gift has made me happier than I have ever been before!"

Then she rode away, hugging the toy in her arms, and Claus, seeing her delight, thought he would make another dolly, better and more natural than the first.

He brought more clay from the brook, and remembering that Bessie had called the dolly her baby he resolved to form this one into a baby's image. That was no difficult task to the clever workman, and soon the baby dolly was lying on the board and placed in the sun to dry. Then, with the clay that was left, he began to make an image of Bessie Blithesome herself.

This was not so easy, for he found he could not make the silken robe of the lord's daughter out of the common clay. So he called the Fairies to his aid, and asked them to bring him colored silks with which to make a real dress for the clay image. The Fairies set off at once on their errand, and before nightfall they returned with a generous supply of silks and laces and golden threads.

Claus now became impatient to complete his new dolly, and instead of waiting for the next day's sun he placed the clay image upon his hearth and covered it over with glowing coals. By morning, when he drew the dolly from the ashes, it had baked as hard as if it had lain a full day in the hot sun.

Now our Claus became a dressmaker as well as a toymaker. He cut the lavender silk, and nearly sewed it into a beautiful gown that just fitted the new dolly. And he put a lace collar around its neck and pink silk shoes on its feet. The natural color of baked clay is a light gray, but Claus painted the face to resemble the color of flesh, and he gave the dolly Bessie's brown eyes and golden hair and rosy cheeks.

It was really a beautiful thing to look upon, and sure to bring joy to some childish heart. While Claus was admiring it he heard a knock at his door, and little Mayrie entered. Her face was sad and her eyes red with continued weeping.

"Why, what has grieved you, my dear?" asked Claus, taking the child in his arms.

"I've—I've—bwoke my tat!" sobbed Mayrie.

"How?" he inquired, his eyes twinkling.

"I—I dwopped him, an' bwoke off him's tail; an'—an'—then I dwopped him an' bwoke off him's ear! An'—an' now him's all spoilt!"

Claus laughed.

"Never mind, Mayrie dear," he said. "How would you like this new dolly, instead of a cat?"

Mayrie looked at the silk-robed dolly and her eyes grew big with astonishment.

"Oh, Tlaus!" she cried, clapping her small hands together with rapture; "tan I have 'at boo'ful lady?"

"Do you like it?" he asked.

"I love it!" said she. "It's better 'an tats!"

"Then take it, dear, and be careful not to break it."

Mayrie took the dolly with a joy that was almost reverent, and her face dimpled with smiles as she started along the path toward home.

6. The Wickedness of the Awgwas

I must now tell you something about the Awgwas, that terrible race of creatures which caused our good Claus so much trouble and nearly succeeded in robbing the children of the world of their earliest and best friend.

I do not like to mention the Awgwas, but they are a part of this history, and cannot be ignored. They were neither mortals nor immortals, but stood midway between those classes of beings. The Awgwas were invisible to ordinary people, but not to immortals. They could pass swiftly through the air from one part of the world to another, and had the power of influencing the minds of human beings to do their wicked will.

They were of gigantic stature and had coarse, scowling countenances which showed plainly their hatred of all mankind. They possessed no consciences whatever and delighted only in evil deeds.

Their homes were in rocky, mountainous places, from whence they sallied forth to accomplish their wicked purposes.

The one of their number that could think of the most horrible deed for them to do was always elected the King Awgwa, and all the race obeyed his orders. Sometimes these creatures lived to become a hundred years old, but usually they fought so fiercely among themselves that many were destroyed in combat, and when they died that was the end of them. Mortals were powerless to harm them and the immortals shuddered when the Awgwas were mentioned, and always avoided them. So they flourished for many years unopposed and accomplished much evil.

I am glad to assure you that these vile creatures have long since perished and passed from earth; but in the days when Claus was making his first toys they were a numerous and powerful tribe.

One of the principal sports of the Awgwas was to inspire angry passions in the hearts of little children, so that they quarreled and fought with one another. They would tempt boys to eat of unripe fruit, and then delight in the pain they suffered; they urged little girls to disobey their parents, and then would laugh when the children were punished. I do not know what causes a child to be naughty in these days, but when the Awgwas were on earth naughty children were usually under their influence.

Now, when Claus began to make children happy he kept them out of the power of the Awgwas; for children possessing such lovely playthings as he gave them had no wish to obey the evil thoughts the Awgwas tried to thrust into their minds.

Therefore, one year when the wicked tribe was to elect a new King, they chose an Awgwa who proposed to destroy Claus and take him away from the children.

"There are, as you know, fewer naughty children in the world since Claus came to the Laughing Valley and began to make his toys," said the new King, as he squatted upon a rock and looked around at the scowling faces of his people. "Why, Bessie Blithesome has not stamped her foot once this month, nor has Mayrie's brother slapped his sister's face or thrown the puppy into the rain-barrel. Little Weekum took his bath last night without screaming or struggling, because his mother had promised he should take his toy cat to bed with him! Such a condition of affairs is awful for any Awgwa to think of, and the only way we can direct the naughty actions of children is to take this person Claus away from them."

"Good! good!" cried the big Awgwas, in a chorus, and they clapped their hands to applaud the speech of the King.

"But what shall we do with him?" asked one of the creatures.

"I have a plan," replied the wicked King; and what his plan was you will soon discover.

That night Claus went to bed feeling very

happy, for he had completed no less than four pretty toys during the day, and they were sure, he thought, to make four little children happy. But while he slept the band of invisible Awgwas surrounded his bed, bound him with stout cords, and then flew away with him to the middle of a dark forest in far off Ethop, where they laid him down and left him.

When morning came Claus found himself thousands of miles from any human being, a prisoner in the wild jungle of an unknown land.

From the limb of a tree above his head swayed a huge python, one of those reptiles that are able to crush a man's bones in their coils. A few yards away crouched a savage panther, its glaring red eyes fixed full on the helpless Claus. One of those monstrous spotted spiders whose sting is death crept stealthily toward him over the matted leaves, which shriveled and turned black at its very touch.

But Claus had been reared in Burzee, and was not afraid.

"Come to me, ye Knooks of the Forest!" he

cried, and gave the low, peculiar whistle that the Knooks know.

The panther, which was about to spring upon its victim, turned and slunk away. The python swung itself into the tree and disappeared among the leaves. The spider stopped short in its advance and hid beneath a rotting log.

Claus had no time to notice them, for he was surrounded by a band of harsh-featured Knooks, more crooked and deformed in appearance than any he had ever seen.

"Who are you that call on us?" demanded one, in a gruff voice.

"The friend of your brothers in Burzee," answered Claus. "I have been brought here by my enemies, the Awgwas, and left to perish miserably. Yet now I implore your help to release me and to send me home again."

"Have you the sign?" asked another.

"Yes," said Claus.

They cut his bonds, and with his free arms he made the secret sign of the Knooks.

Instantly they assisted him to stand upon his

feet, and they brought him food and drink to strengthen him.

"Our brothers of Burzee make queer friends," grumbled an ancient Knook whose flowing beard was pure white. "But he who knows our secret sign and signal is entitled to our help, whoever he may be. Close your eyes, stranger, and we will conduct you to your home. Where shall we seek it?"

"'Tis in the Laughing Valley," answered Claus, shutting his eyes.

"There is but one Laughing Valley in the known world, so we cannot go astray," remarked the Knook.

As he spoke the sound of his voice seemed to die away, so Claus opened his eyes to see what caused the change. To his astonishment he found himself seated on the bench by his own door, with the Laughing Valley spread out before him. That day he visited the Wood-Nymphs and related his adventure to Queen Zurline and Necile.

"The Awgwas have become your enemies," said the lovely Queen, thoughtfully, "so we must do all we can to protect you from their power."

"It was cowardly to bind him while he slept," remarked Necile, with indignation.

"The evil ones are ever cowardly," answered Zurline, "but our friend's slumber shall not be disturbed again."

The Queen herself came to the dwelling of Claus that evening and placed her Seal on every door and window, to keep out the Awgwas. And under the Seal of Queen Zurline was placed the Seal of the Fairies and the Seal of the Ryls and the Seals of the Knooks, that the charm might become more powerful.

And Claus carried his toys to the children again, and made many more of the little ones happy.

You may guess how angry the King Awgwa and his fierce band were when it was known to them that Claus had escaped from the Forest of Ethop.

They raged madly for a whole week, and then held another meeting among the rocks.

"It is useless to carry him where the Knooks reign," said the King, "for he has their protection.

So let us cast him into a cave of our own mountains, where he will surely perish."

This was promptly agreed to, and the wicked band set out that night to seize Claus. But they found his dwelling guarded by the Seals of the Immortals and were obliged to go away baffled and disappointed.

"Never mind," said the King. "He does not sleep always!"

Next day, as Claus traveled to the village across the plain, where he intended to present a toy squirrel to a lame boy, he was suddenly set upon by the Awgwas, who seized him and carried him away to the mountains.

There they thrust him within a deep cavern and rolled many huge rocks against the entrance to prevent his escape.

Deprived thus of light and food, and with little air to breathe, our Claus was, indeed, in a pitiful plight. But he spoke the mystic words of the Fairies, which always command their friendly aid, and they came to his rescue and transported him to the Laughing Valley in the twinkling of an eye.

Thus the Awgwas discovered they might not destroy one who had earned the friendship of the immortals; so the evil band sought other means of keeping Claus from bringing happiness to children and so making them obedient.

Whenever Claus set out to carry his toys to the little ones an Awgwa, who had been set to watch his movements, sprang upon him and snatched the toys from his grasp. And the children were no more disappointed than was Claus when he was obliged to return home disconsolate. Still he persevered, and made many toys for his little friends and started with them for the villages. And always the Awgwas robbed him as soon as he had left the Valley.

They threw the stolen playthings into one of their lonely caverns, and quite a heap of toys accumulated before Claus became discouraged and gave up all attempts to leave the Valley. Then children began coming to him, since they found he did not go to them; but the wicked Awgwas flew around them and caused their steps to stray and the paths to become crooked, so never a little one could find a way into the Laughing Valley.

Lonely days now fell upon Claus, for he was denied the pleasure of bringing happiness to the children whom he had learned to love. Yet he bore up bravely, for he thought surely the time would come when the Awgwas would abandon their evil designs to injure him.

He devoted all his hours to toy-making, and when one plaything had been completed he stood it on a shelf he had built for that purpose. When the shelf became filled with rows of toys he made another one, and filled that also. So that in time he had many shelves filled with gay and beautiful toys representing horses, dogs, cats, elephants, lambs, rabbits and deer, as well as pretty dolls of all sizes and balls and marbles of baked clay painted in gay colors.

Often, as he glanced at this array of child-ish treasures, the heart of good old Claus became sad, so greatly did he long to carry the toys to his children. And at last, because he could bear it no longer, he ventured to go to the great Ak, to whom he told the story of his persecution by the Awgwas, and begged the Master Woodsman to assist him.

7. The Great Battle Between Good and Evil

Ak listened gravely to the recital of Claus, stroking his beard the while with the slow, graceful motion that betokened deep thought. He nodded approvingly when Claus told how the Knooks and Fairies had saved him from death, and frowned when he heard how the Awgwas had stolen the children's toys. At last he said: "From the beginning I have approved the work you are doing among the children of men, and it annoys me that your good deeds should be thwarted by the Awgwas. We immortals have no connection whatever with the evil creatures who have attacked you. Always have we avoided them, and they, in turn, have hitherto taken care not to cross our pathway. But in this matter I find they have interfered with one of our friends, and I will ask them to abandon their persecutions, as you are under our protection."

Claus thanked the Master Woodsman most gratefully and returned to his Valley, while Ak, who never delayed carrying out his promises, at once traveled to the mountains of the Awgwas.

There, standing on the bare rocks, he called on the King and his people to appear.

Instantly the place was filled with throngs of the scowling Awgwas, and their King, perching himself on a point of rock, demanded fiercely: "Who dares call on us?"

"It is I, the Master Woodsman of the World," responded Ak.

"Here are no forests for you to claim," cried the King, angrily. "We owe no allegiance to you, nor to any immortal!"

"That is true," replied Ak, calmly. "Yet you have ventured to interfere with the actions of Claus, who dwells in the Laughing Valley, and is under our protection."

Many of the Awgwas began muttering at this speech, and their King turned threateningly on the Master Woodsman.

"You are set to rule the forests, but the plains and the valleys are ours!" he shouted. "Keep to your own dark woods! We will do as we please with Claus."

"You shall not harm our friend in any way!" replied Ak.

"Shall we not?" asked the King, impudently. "You will see! Our powers are vastly superior to those of mortals, and fully as great as those of immortals."

"It is your conceit that misleads you!" said Ak, sternly. "You are a transient race, passing from life into nothingness. We, who live forever, pity but despise you. On earth you are scorned by all, and in Heaven you have no place! Even the mortals, after their earth life, enter another existence for all time, and so are your superiors. How then dare you, who are neither mortal nor immortal, refuse to obey my wish?"

The Awgwas sprang to their feet with menacing gestures, but their King motioned them back.

"Never before," he cried to Ak, while his voice trembled with rage, "has an immortal declared himself the master of the Awgwas! Never shall an immortal venture to interfere with our actions again! For we will avenge your scornful words by killing your friend Claus within three days. Nor you, nor all the immortals can save him from our wrath. We defy your powers! Begone, Master Woodsman of the World! In the country of the Awgwas you have no place."

"It is war!" declared Ak, with flashing eyes.

"It is war!" returned the King, savagely. "In three days your friend will be dead."

The Master turned away and came to his Forest of Burzee, where he called a meeting of the immortals and told them of the defiance of the Awgwas and their purpose to kill Claus within three days.

The little folk listened to him quietly.

"What shall we do?" asked Ak.

"These creatures are of no benefit to the world," said the Prince of the Knooks. "We must destroy them."

"Their lives are devoted only to evil deeds," said the Prince of the Ryls. "We must destroy them."

"They have no conscience, and endeavor to

make all mortals as bad as themselves," said the Queen of the Fairies. "We must destroy them."

"They have defied the great Ak, and threaten the life of our adopted son," said beautiful Queen Zurline. "We must destroy them."

The Master Woodsman smiled.

"You speak well," said he. "These Awgwas we know to be a powerful race, and they will fight desperately; yet the outcome is certain. For we who live can never die, even though conquered by our enemies, while every Awgwa who is struck down is one foe the less to oppose us. Prepare, then, for battle, and let us resolve to show no mercy to the wicked!"

Thus arose that terrible war between the immortals and the spirits of evil which is sung of in Fairyland to this very day.

The King Awgwa and his band determined to carry out the threat to destroy Claus. They now hated him for two reasons: he made children happy and was a friend of the Master Woodsman. But since Ak's visit they had reason to fear the opposition of the immortals, and they dreaded l

defeat. So the King sent swift messengers to all parts of the world to summon every evil creature to his aid.

And on the third day after the declaration of war a mighty army was at the command of the King Awgwa. There were three hundred Asiatic Dragons, breathing fire that consumed everything it touched. These hated mankind and all good spirits. And there were the three-eyed Giants of Tatary, a host in themselves, who liked nothing better than to fight. And next came the Black Demons from Patalonia, with great spreading wings like those of a bat, which swept terror and misery through the world as they beat upon the air. And joined to these were the Goozzle-Goblins, with long talons as sharp as swords, with which they clawed the flesh from their foes. Finally, every mountain Awgwa in the world had come to participate in the great battle with the immortals.

The King Awgwa looked around upon this vast army and his heart beat high with wicked pride, for he believed he would surely triumph over his gentle enemies, who had never before been known to fight. But the Master Woodsman had not been idle. None of his people was used to warfare, yet now that they were called upon to face the hosts of evil they willingly prepared for the fray.

Ak had commanded them to assemble in the Laughing Valley, where Claus, ignorant of the terrible battle that was to be waged on his account, was quietly making his toys.

Soon the entire Valley, from hill to hill, was filled with the little immortals. The Master Woodsman stood first, bearing a gleaming ax that shone like burnished silver. Next came the Ryls, armed with sharp thorns from bramblebushes. Then the Knooks, bearing the spears they used when they were forced to prod their savage beasts into submission. The Fairies, dressed in white gauze with rainbow-hued wings, bore golden wands, and the Wood-nymphs, in their uniforms of oak-leaf green, carried switches from ash trees as weapons.

Loud laughed the Awgwa King when he beheld the size and the arms of his foes. To be sure the mighty ax of the Woodsman was to be dreaded, but the sweet-faced Nymphs and pretty Fairies, the gentle Ryls and crooked Knooks were such harmless folk that he almost felt shame at having called such a terrible host to oppose them.

"Since these fools dare fight," he said to the leader of the Tatary Giants, "I will overwhelm them with our evil powers!"

To begin the battle he poised a great stone in his left hand and cast it full against the sturdy form of the Master Woodsman, who turned it aside with his ax. Then rushed the three-eyed Giants of Tatary upon the Knooks, and the Goozzle-Goblins upon the Ryls, and the fire-breathing Dragons upon the sweet Fairies. Because the Nymphs were Ak's own people the band of Awgwas sought them out, thinking to overcome them with ease.

But it is the Law that while Evil, unopposed, may accomplish terrible deeds, the powers of Good can never be overthrown when opposed to Evil. Well had it been for the King Awgwa had he known the Law!

His ignorance cost him his existence, for one flash of the ax borne by the Master Woodsman of the World cleft the wicked King in twain and rid the earth of the vilest creature it contained.

Greatly marveled the Tatary Giants when the spears of the little Knooks pierced their thick walls of flesh and sent them reeling to the ground with howls of agony.

Woe came upon the sharp-taloned Goblins when the thorns of the Ryls reached their savage hearts and let their life-blood sprinkle all the plain. And afterward from every drop a thistle grew.

The Dragons paused astonished before the Fairy wands, from whence rushed a power that caused their fiery breaths to flow back on themselves so that they shriveled away and died.

As for the Awgwas, they had scant time to realize how they were destroyed, for the ash switches of the Nymphs bore a charm unknown to any Awgwa, and turned their foes into clods of earth at the slightest touch!

When Ak leaned upon his gleaming ax and

turned to look over the field of battle he saw the few Giants who were able to run disappearing over the distant hills on their return to Tatary. The Goblins had perished every one, as had the terrible Dragons, while all that remained of the wicked Awgwas was a great number of earthen hillocks dotting the plain.

And now the immortals melted from the Valley like dew at sunrise, to resume their duties in the Forest, while Ak walked slowly and thoughtfully to the house of Claus and entered.

"You have many toys ready for the children," said the Woodsman, "and now you may carry them across the plain to the dwellings and the villages without fear."

"Will not the Awgwas harm me?" asked Claus, eagerly.

"The Awgwas," said Ak, "have perished!"

.   .   .

Now I will gladly have done with wicked spirits and with fighting and bloodshed. It was not from choice that I told of the Awgwas and their allies, and of their great battle with the immortals. They were part of this history, and could not be avoided.

8. The First Journey with the Reindeer

Those were happy days for Claus when he carried his accumulation of toys to the children who had awaited them so long. During his imprisonment in the Valley he had been so industrious that all his shelves were filled with playthings, and after quickly supplying the little ones living nearby he saw he must now extend his travels to wider fields.

Remembering the time when he had journeyed with Ak through all the world, he knew children were everywhere, and he longed to make as many as possible happy with his gifts.

So he loaded a great sack with all kinds of toys, slung it upon his back that he might carry it more easily, and started off on a longer trip than he had yet undertaken.

Wherever he showed his merry face, in

hamlet or in farmhouse, he received a cordial welcome, for his fame had spread into far lands. At each village the children swarmed about him, following his footsteps wherever he went; and the women thanked him gratefully for the joy he brought their little ones; and the men looked upon him curiously that he should devote his time to such a queer occupation as toy-making. But every one smiled on him and gave him kindly words, and Claus felt amply repaid for his long journey.

When the sack was empty he went back again to the Laughing Valley and once more filled it to the brim. This time he followed another road, into a different part of the country, and carried happiness to many children who never before had owned a toy or guessed that such a delightful plaything existed.

After a third journey, so far away that Claus was many days walking the distance, the store of toys became exhausted and without delay he set about making a fresh supply.

From seeing so many children and studying

their tastes he had acquired several new ideas about toys.

The dollies were, he had found, the most delightful of all playthings for babies and little girls, and often those who could not say "dolly" would call for a "doll" in their sweet baby talk. So Claus resolved to make many dolls, of all sizes, and to dress them in bright-colored clothing. The older boys—and even some of the girls—loved the images of animals, so he still made cats and elephants and horses. And many of the little fellows had musical natures, and longed for drums and cymbals and whistles and horns. So he made a number of toy drums, with tiny sticks to beat them with; and he made whistles from the willow trees, and horns from the bog-reeds, and cymbals from bits of beaten metal.

All this kept him busily at work, and before he realized it the winter season came, with deeper snows than usual, and he knew he could not leave the Valley with his heavy pack. Moreover, the next trip would take him farther from home than ever before, and Jack Frost was mischievous enough to nip his nose and ears if he undertook the long journey while the Frost King reigned. The Frost King was Jack's father and never reproved him for his pranks.

So Claus remained at his work-bench; but he whistled and sang as merrily as ever, for he would allow no disappointment to sour his temper or make him unhappy.

One bright morning he looked from his window and saw two of the deer he had known in the Forest walking toward his house.

Claus was surprised; not that the friendly deer should visit him, but that they walked on the surface of the snow as easily as if it were solid ground, notwithstanding the fact that throughout the Valley the snow lay many feet deep. He had walked out of his house a day or two before and had sunk to his armpits in a drift.

So when the deer came near he opened the door and called to them: "Good morning, Flossie! Tell me how you are able to walk on the snow so easily."

"It is frozen hard," answered Flossie.

"The Frost King has breathed on it," said

Glossie, coming up, "and the surface is now as solid as ice."

"Perhaps," remarked Claus, thoughtfully, "I might now carry my pack of toys to the children."

"Is it a long journey?" asked Flossie.

"Yes; it will take me many days, for the pack is heavy," answered Claus.

"Then the snow would melt before you could get back," said the deer. "You must wait until spring, Claus."

Claus sighed. "Had I your fleet feet," said he, "I could make the journey in a day."

"But you have not," returned Glossie, looking at his own slender legs with pride.

"Perhaps I could ride upon your back," Claus ventured to remark, after a pause.

"Oh no; our backs are not strong enough to bear your weight," said Flossie, decidedly. "But if you had a sledge, and could harness us to it, we might draw you easily, and your pack as well."

"I'll make a sledge!" exclaimed Claus. "Will you agree to draw me if I do?"

"Well," replied Flossie, "we must first go and

ask the Knooks, who are our guardians, for permission; but if they consent, and you can make a sledge and harness, we will gladly assist you."

"Then go at once!" cried Claus, eagerly. "I am sure the friendly Knooks will give their consent, and by the time you are back I shall be ready to harness you to my sledge."

Flossie and Glossie, being deer of much intelligence, had long wished to see the great world, so they gladly ran over the frozen snow to ask the Knooks if they might carry Claus on his journey.

Meantime the toy-maker hurriedly began the construction of a sledge, using material from his wood-pile. He made two long runners that turned upward at the front ends, and across these nailed short boards, to make a platform. It was soon completed, but was as rude in appearance as it is possible for a sledge to be.

The harness was more difficult to prepare, but Claus twisted strong cords together and knotted them so they would fit around the necks of the deer, in the shape of a collar. From these ran other cords to fasten the deer to the front of the sledge.

Before the work was completed Glossie and Flossie were back from the Forest, having been granted permission by Will Knook to make the journey with Claus provided they would to Burzee by daybreak the next morning.

"That is not a very long time," said Flossie; "but we are swift and strong, and if we get started by this evening we can travel many miles during the night."

Claus decided to make the attempt, so he hurried on his preparations as fast as possible. After a time he fastened the collars around the necks of his steeds and harnessed them to his rude sledge. Then he placed a stool on the little platform, to serve as a seat, and filled a sack with his prettiest toys.

"How do you intend to guide us?" asked Glossie. "We have never been out of the Forest before, except to visit your house, so we shall not know the way."

Claus thought about that for a moment. Then he brought more cords and fastened two of them to the spreading antlers of each deer, one on the right and the other on the left.

"Those will be my reins," said Claus, "and when I pull them to the right or to the left you must go in that direction. If I do not pull the reins at all you may go straight ahead."

"Very well," answered Glossie and Flossie; and then they asked: "Are you ready?"

Claus seated himself upon the stool, placed the sack of toys at his feet, and then gathered up the reins.

"All ready!" he shouted. "Away we go!"

The deer leaned forward, lifted their slender limbs, and the next moment away flew the sledge over the frozen snow. The swiftness of the motion surprised Claus, for in a few strides they were across the Valley and gliding over the broad plain beyond.

The day had melted into evening by the time they started; for, swiftly as Claus had worked, many hours had been consumed in making his preparations. But the moon shone brightly to light their way, and Claus soon decided it was just as pleasant to travel by night as by day.

The deer liked it better; for, although they

wished to see something of the world, they were timid about meeting men, and now all the dwellers in the towns and farmhouses were sound asleep and could not see them.

Away and away they sped, on and on over the hills and through the valleys and across the plains until they reached a village where Claus had never been before.

Here he called on them to stop, and they immediately obeyed. But a new difficulty now presented itself, for the people had locked their doors when they went to bed, and Claus found he could not enter the houses to leave his toys.

"I am afraid, my friends, we have made our journey for nothing," said he, "for I shall be obliged to carry my playthings back home again without giving them to the children of this village."

"What's the matter?" asked Flossie.

"The doors are locked," answered Claus, "and I cannot get in."

Glossie looked around at the houses. The snow was quite deep in that village, and just before them was a roof only a few feet above the sledge. A broad chimney, which seemed to Glossie big enough to admit Claus, was at the peak of the roof.

"Why don't you climb down that chimney?" asked Glossie.

Claus looked at it.

"That would be easy enough if I were on top of the roof," he answered.

"Then hold fast and we will take you there," said the deer, and they gave one bound to the roof and landed beside the big chimney.

"Good!" cried Claus, well pleased, and he slung the pack of toys over his shoulder and got into the chimney.

There was plenty of soot on the bricks, but he did not mind that, and by placing his hands and knees against the sides he crept downward until he had reached the fireplace. Leaping lightly over the smoldering coals he found himself in a large sitting-room, where a dim light was burning.

From this room two doorways led into smaller chambers. In one a woman lay asleep, with a baby beside her in a crib.

Claus laughed, but he did not laugh aloud for fear of waking the baby. Then he slipped a big doll from his pack and laid it in the crib. The little one smiled, as if it dreamed of the pretty plaything it was to find on the morrow, and Claus crept softly from the room and entered at the other doorway.

Here were two boys, fast asleep with their arms around each other's neck. Claus gazed at them lovingly a moment and then placed upon the bed a drum, two horns and a wooden elephant.

He did not linger, now that his work in this house was done, but climbed the chimney again and seated himself on his sledge.

"Can you find another chimney?" he asked the reindeer.

"Easily enough," replied Glossie and Flossie.

Down to the edge of the roof they raced, and then, without pausing, leaped through the air to the top of the next building, where a huge, old-fashioned chimney stood.

"Don't be so long, this time," called Flossie, "or we shall never get back to the Forest by daybreak."

Claus made a trip down this chimney also and found five children sleeping in the house, all of whom were quickly supplied with toys.

When he returned the deer sprang to the next roof, but on descending the chimney Claus found no children there at all. That was not often the case in this village, however, so he lost less time than you might suppose in visiting the dreary homes where there were no little ones.

When he had climbed down the chimneys of all the houses in that village, and had left a toy for every sleeping child, Claus found that his great sack was not yet half emptied.

"Onward, friends!" he called to the deer. "We must seek another village."

So away they dashed, although it was long past midnight, and in a surprisingly short time they came to a large city, the largest Claus had ever visited since he began to make toys. But, nothing daunted by the throng of houses, he set to work at once and his beautiful steeds carried him rapidly from one roof to another, only the highest being beyond the leaps of the agile deer.

At last the supply of toys was exhausted and Claus seated himself in the sledge, with the empty sack at his feet, and turned the heads of Glossie and Flossie toward home.

Presently Flossie asked: "What is that gray streak in the sky?"

"It is the coming dawn of day," answered Claus, surprised to find that it was so late.

"Good gracious!" exclaimed Glossie. "Then we shall not be home by daybreak, and the Knooks will punish us and never let us come again."

"We must race for the Laughing Valley and make our best speed," returned Flossie, "so hold fast, friend Claus!"

Claus held fast and the next moment was flying so swiftly over the snow that he could not see the trees as they whirled past. Up hill and down dale, swift as an arrow shot from a bow they dashed, and Claus shut his eyes to keep the wind out of them and left the deer to find their own way.

It seemed to him they were plunging through space, but he was not at all afraid. The Knooks were severe masters, and must be obeyed at all hazards, and the gray streak in the sky was growing brighter every moment.

Finally the sledge came to a sudden stop and Claus, who was taken unawares, tumbled from his seat into a snowdrift. As he picked himself up he heard the deer crying: "Quick, friend, quick! Cut away our harness!"

He drew his knife and rapidly severed the cords, and then he wiped the moisture from his eyes and looked around him.

The sledge had come to a stop in the Laughing Valley, only a few feet, he found, from his own door. In the East the day was breaking, and turning to the edge of Burzee he saw Glossie and Flossie just disappearing in the Forest.

9. "Santa Claus!"

Claus thought that none of the children would ever know where the toys came from which they found by their bedsides when they wakened the following morning. But kindly deeds are sure to bring fame, and fame has many wings to carry its tidings into far lands; so for miles and miles in every direction people were talking of Claus and his wonderful gifts to children. The sweet generousness of his work caused a few selfish folk to sneer, but even these were forced to admit their respect for a man so gentle-natured that he loved to devote his life to pleasing the helpless little ones of his race.

Therefore the inhabitants of every city and village had been eagerly watching the coming of Claus, and remarkable stories of his beautiful playthings were told the children to keep them patient and contented.

When, on the morning following the first trip of Claus with his deer, the little ones came running to their parents with the pretty toys they had found, and asked from whence they came, there was but one reply to the question.

"The good Claus must have been here, my darlings; for his are the only toys in all the world!"

"But how did he get in?" asked the children.

At this the fathers shook their heads, being themselves unable to understand how Claus had gained admittance to their homes; but the mothers, watching the glad faces of their dear ones, whispered that the good Claus was no mortal man but assuredly a Saint, and they piously blessed his name for the happiness he had bestowed upon their children.

"A Saint," said one, with bowed head, "has no need to unlock doors if it pleases him to enter our homes."

And, afterward, when a child was naughty or disobedient, its mother would say: "You must pray to the good Santa Claus for forgiveness. He does not like naughty children, and, unless you repent, he will bring you no more pretty toys."

But Santa Claus himself would not have approved this speech. He brought toys to the children because they were little and helpless, and because he loved them. He knew that the best of children were sometimes naughty, and that the naughty ones were often good. It is the way with children, the world over, and he would not have changed their natures had he possessed the power to do so.

And that is how our Claus became Santa

Claus. It is possible for any man, by good deeds, to enshrine himself as a Saint in the hearts of the people.

10. Christmas Eve

The day that broke as Claus returned from his night ride with Glossie and Flossie brought to him a new trouble. Will Knook, the chief guardian of the deer, came to him, surly and ill-tempered, to complain that he had kept Glossie and Flossie beyond daybreak, in opposition to his orders.

"Yet it could not have been very long after daybreak," said Claus.

"It was one minute after," answered Will Knook, "and that is as bad as one hour. I shall set the stinging gnats on Glossie and Flossie, and they will thus suffer terribly for their disobedience."

"Don't do that!" begged Claus. "It was my fault."

But Will Knook would listen to no excuses, and went away grumbling and growling in his ill-natured way.

For this reason Claus entered the Forest to consult Necile about rescuing the good deer from punishment. To his delight he found his old friend, the Master Woodsman, seated in the circle of Nymphs.

Ak listened to the story of the night journey to the children and of the great assistance the deer had been to Claus by drawing his sledge over the frozen snow.

"I do not wish my friends to be punished if I can save them," said the toy-maker, when he had finished the relation. "They were only one minute late, and they ran swifter than a bird flies to get home before daybreak."

Ak stroked his beard thoughtfully a moment, and then sent for the Prince of the Knooks, who rules all his people in Burzee, and also for the Queen of the Fairies and the Prince of the Ryls.

When all had assembled Claus told his story again, at Ak's command, and then the Master addressed the Prince of the Knooks, saying: "The good work that Claus is doing among mankind deserves the support of every honest immortal. Already he is called a Saint in some of the towns, and before long the name of Santa Claus will be lovingly known in every home that is blessed with children. Moreover, he is a son of our Forest, so we owe him our encouragement. You, Ruler of the Knooks, have known him these many years; am I not right in saying he deserves our friendship?"

The Prince, crooked and sour of visage as all Knooks are, looked only upon the dead leaves at his feet and muttered: "You are the Master Woodsman of the World!"

Ak smiled, but continued, in soft tones: "It seems that the deer which are guarded by your people can be of great assistance to Claus, and as they seem willing to draw his sledge I beg that you will permit him to use their services whenever he pleases."

The Prince did not reply, but tapped the curled point of his sandal with the tip of his spear, as if in thought.

Then the Fairy Queen spoke to him in this way: "If you consent to Ak's request I will see that no harm comes to your deer while they are away from the Forest."

And the Prince of the Ryls added: "For my part I will allow to every deer that assists Claus the privilege of eating my casa plants, which give strength, and my grawle plants, which give fleetness of foot, and my marbon plants, which give long life."

And the Queen of the Nymphs said: "The deer which draw the sledge of Claus will be permitted to bathe in the Forest pool of Nares, which will give them sleek coats and wonderful beauty."

The Prince of the Knooks, hearing these promises, shifted uneasily on his seat, for in his heart he hated to refuse a request of his fellow immortals, although they were asking an unusual favor at his hands, and the Knooks are unaccustomed to granting favors of any kind. Finally he turned to his servants and said:

"Call Will Knook."

When surly Will came and heard the demands of the immortals he protested loudly against granting them.

"Deer are deer," said he, "and nothing but deer. Were they horses it would be right to harness them like horses. But no one harnesses deer because they are free, wild creatures, owing no service of any sort to mankind. It would degrade my deer to labor for Claus, who is only a man in spite of the friendship lavished on him by the immortals."

"You have heard," said the Prince to Ak. "There is truth in what Will says."

"Call Glossie and Flossie," returned the Master.

The deer were brought to the conference and Ak asked them if they objected to drawing the sledge for Claus.

"No, indeed!" replied Glossie. "We enjoyed the trip very much."

"And we tried to get home by daybreak," added Flossie, "but were unfortunately a minute too late."

"A minute lost at daybreak doesn't matter," said Ak. "You are forgiven for that delay."

"Provided it does not happen again," said the Prince of the Knooks, sternly.

"And will you permit them to make another journey with me?" asked Claus, eagerly.

The Prince reflected while he gazed at Will, who was scowling, and at the Master Woodsman, who was smiling.

Then he stood up and addressed the company as follows: "Since you all urge me to grant the favor I will permit the deer to go with Claus once every year, on Christmas Eve, provided they always return to the Forest by daybreak. He may select any number he pleases, up to ten, to draw his sledge, and those shall be known among us as Reindeer, to distinguish them from the others. And they shall bathe in the Pool of Nares, and eat the casa and grawle and marbon plants and shall be under the especial protection of the Fairy Queen. And now cease scowling, Will Knook, for my words shall be obeyed!"

He hobbled quickly away through the trees, to avoid the thanks of Claus and the approval of the other immortals, and Will, looking as cross as ever, followed him.

But Ak was satisfied, knowing that he could

rely on the promise of the Prince, however grudgingly given; and Glossie and Flossie ran home, kicking up their heels delightedly at every step.

"When is Christmas Eve?" Claus asked the Master.

"In about ten days," he replied.

"Then I cannot use the deer this year," said Claus, thoughtfully, "for I shall not have time enough to make my sackful of toys."

"The shrewd Prince foresaw that," responded Ak, "and therefore named Christmas Eve as the day you might use the deer, knowing it would cause you to lose an entire year."

"If I only had the toys the Awgwas stole from me," said Claus, sadly, "I could easily fill my sack for the children."

"Where are they?" asked the Master.

"I do not know," replied Claus, "but the wicked Awgwas probably hid them in the mountains."

Ak turned to the Fairy Queen.

"Can you find them?" he asked.

"I will try," she replied, brightly.

Then Claus went back to the Laughing Valley,

to work as hard as he could, and a band of Fairies immediately flew to the mountain that had been haunted by the Awgwas and began a search for the stolen toys.

The Fairies, as we well know, possess wonderful powers; but the cunning Awgwas had hidden the toys in a deep cave and covered the opening with rocks, so no one could look in. Therefore all search for the missing playthings proved in vain for several days, and Claus, who sat at home waiting for news from the Fairies, almost despaired of getting the toys before Christmas Eve.

He worked hard every moment, but it took considerable time to carve out and to shape each toy and to paint it properly, so that on the morning before Christmas Eve only half of one small shelf above the window was filled with playthings ready for the children.

But on this morning the Fairies who were searching in the mountains had a new thought. They joined hands and moved in a straight line through the rocks that formed the mountain, beginning at the topmost peak and working downward, so that no spot could be missed by their bright eyes. And at last they discovered the cave where the toys had been heaped up by the wicked Awgwas.

It did not take them long to burst open the mouth of the cave, and then each one seized as many toys as he could carry and they all flew to Claus and laid the treasure before him.

The good man was rejoiced to receive, just in the nick of time, such a store of playthings with which to load his sledge, and he sent word to Glossie and Flossie to be ready for the journey at nightfall.

With all his other labors he had managed to find time, since the last trip, to repair the harness and to strengthen his sledge, so that when the deer came to him at twilight he had no difficulty in harnessing them.

"We must go in another direction to-night," he told them, "where we shall find children I have never yet visited. And we must travel fast and work quickly, for my sack is full of toys and running over the brim!"

So, just as the moon arose, they dashed out of the Laughing Valley and across the plain and over the hills to the south. The air was sharp and frosty and the starlight touched the snowflakes and made them glitter like countless diamonds. The reindeer leaped onward with strong, steady bounds, and Claus' heart was so light and merry that he laughed and sang while the wind whistled past his ears:

"With a ho, ho, ho!
And a ha, ha, ha!
And a ho, ho! ha, ha, hee!
Now away we go
O'er the frozen snow,
As merry as we can be!"

Jack Frost heard him and came racing up with his nippers, but when he saw it was Claus he laughed and turned away again.

The mother owls heard him as he passed near a wood and stuck their heads out of the hollow places in the tree trunks; but when they saw who it was they whispered to the owlets nestling near them that it was only Santa Claus carrying toys to the children. It is strange how much those mother owls know.

Claus stopped at some of the scattered farmhouses and climbed down the chimneys to leave presents for the babies. Soon after he reached a village and worked merrily for an hour distributing playthings among the sleeping little ones. Then away again he went, singing his joyous carol:

"Now away we go
O'er the gleaming snow,
While the deer run swift and free!
For to girls and boys
We carry the toys
That will fill their hearts with glee!"

The deer liked the sound of his deep bass voice and kept time to the song with their hoofbeats on the hard snow; but soon they stopped at another chimney and Santa Claus, with sparkling eyes and face brushed red by the wind, climbed down its smoky sides and left a present for every child the house contained.

It was a merry, happy night. Swiftly the deer ran, and busily their driver worked to scatter his gifts among the sleeping children.

But the sack was empty at last, and the sledge headed homeward; and now again the race with daybreak began. Glossie and Flossie had no mind to be rebuked a second time for tardiness, so they fled with a swiftness that enabled them to pass the gale on which the Frost King rode, and soon brought them to the Laughing Valley.

It is true when Claus released his steeds from their harness the eastern sky was streaked with gray, but Glossie and Flossie were deep in the Forest before day fairly broke.

Claus was so wearied with his night's work that he threw himself upon his bed and fell into a deep slumber, and while he slept the Christmas sun appeared in the sky and shone upon hundreds of happy homes where the sound of childish laughter proclaimed that Santa Claus had made them a visit.

God bless him! It was his first Christmas Eve, and for hundreds of years since then he has nobly fulfilled his mission to bring happiness to the hearts of little children.

11. How the First Stockings Were Hung by the Chimneys

When you remember that no child, until Santa Claus began his travels, had ever known the pleasure of possessing a toy, you will understand how joy crept into the homes of those who had been favored with a visit from the good man, and how they talked of him day by day in loving tones and were honestly grateful for his kindly deeds. It is true that great warriors and mighty kings and clever scholars of that day were often spoken of by the people; but no one of them was so greatly beloved as Santa Claus, because none other was so unselfish as to devote himself to making others happy. For a generous deed lives longer than a great battle or a king's decree of a scholar's essay, because it spreads and leaves its mark on all nature and endures through many generations.

The bargain made with the Knook Prince changed the plans of Claus for all future time; for, being able to use the reindeer on but one night of each year, he decided to devote all the other days to the manufacture of playthings, and on Christmas Eve to carry them to the children of the world.

But a year's work would, he knew, result in a vast accumulation of toys, so he resolved to build a new sledge that would be larger and stronger and better-fitted for swift travel than the old and clumsy one.

His first act was to visit the Gnome King, with whom he made a bargain to exchange three drums, a trumpet and two dolls for a pair of fine steel runners, curled beautifully at the ends. For the Gnome King had children of his own, who, living in the hollows under the earth, in mines and caverns, needed something to amuse them.

In three days the steel runners were ready, and when Claus brought the playthings to the Gnome King, his Majesty was so greatly pleased with them that he presented Claus with a string of sweet-toned sleigh-bells, in addition to the runners.

"These will please Glossie and Flossie," said Claus, as he jingled the bells and listened to their merry sound. "But I should have two strings of bells, one for each deer."

"Bring me another trumpet and a toy cat," replied the King, "and you shall have a second string of bells like the first."

"It is a bargain!" cried Claus, and he went home again for the toys.

The new sledge was carefully built, the Knooks bringing plenty of strong but thin boards to use in its construction. Claus made a high, rounding dash-board to keep off the snow cast behind by the fleet hoofs of the deer; and he made high sides to the platform so that many toys could be carried, and finally he mounted the sledge upon the slender steel runners made by the Gnome King.

It was certainly a handsome sledge, and big and roomy. Claus painted it in bright colors, although no one was likely to see it during his midnight journeys, and when all was finished he sent for Glossie and Flossie to come and look at it.

The deer admired the sledge, but gravely declared it was too big and heavy for them to draw.

"We might pull it over the snow, to be sure," said Glossie; "but we would not pull it fast enough to enable us to visit the far-away cities and villages and return to the Forest by daybreak."

"Then I must add two more deer to my team," declared Claus, after a moment's thought.

"The Knook Prince allowed you as many as ten. Why not use them all?" asked Flossie. "Then we could speed like the lightning and leap to the highest roofs with ease."

"A team of ten reindeer!" cried Claus, delightedly. "That will be splendid. Please return to the Forest at once and select eight other deer as like yourselves as possible. And you must all eat of the casa plant, to become strong, and of the grawle plant, to become fleet of foot, and of the marbon plant, that you may live long to accompany me on my journeys. Likewise it will be well for you to bathe in the Pool of Nares, which the lovely Queen Zurline declares will render you rarely beautiful. Should you perform these duties faithfully there is no doubt that on next Christmas Eve my ten reindeer will be the most powerful and beautiful steeds the world has ever seen!"

So Glossie and Flossie went to the Forest to choose their mates, and Claus began to consider the question of a harness for them all.

In the end he called upon Peter Knook for assistance, for Peter's heart is as kind as his body is crooked, and he is remarkably shrewd, as well. And Peter agreed to furnish strips of tough leather for the harness.

This leather was cut from the skins of lions that had reached such an advanced age that they died naturally, and on one side was tawny hair while the other side was cured to the softness of velvet by the deft Knooks. When Claus received these strips of leather he sewed them neatly into a harness for the ten reindeer, and it proved strong and serviceable and lasted him for many years.

The harness and sledge were prepared at odd

times, for Claus devoted most of his days to the making of toys. These were now much better than the first ones had been, for the immortals often came to his house to watch him work and to offer suggestions. It was Necile's idea to make some of the dolls say "papa" and "mama." It was a thought of the Knooks to put a squeak inside the lambs, so that when a child squeezed them they would say "baa-a-a-a!" And the Fairy Queen advised Claus to put whistles in the birds, so they could be made to sing, and wheels on the horses, so children could draw them around. Many animals perished in the Forest, from one cause or another, and their fur was brought to Claus that he might cover with it the small images of beasts he made for playthings. A merry Ryl suggested that Claus make a donkey with a nodding head, which he did, and afterward found that it amused the little ones immensely. And so the toys grew in beauty and attractiveness every day, until they were the wonder of even the immortals.

When another Christmas Eve drew near there was a monster load of beautiful gifts for the children ready to be loaded upon the big sledge. Claus filled three sacks to the brim, and tucked every corner of the sledge-box full of toys besides.

Then, at twilight, the ten reindeer appeared and Flossie introduced them all to Claus. They were Racer and Pacer, Reckless and Speckless, Fearless and Peerless, and Ready and Steady, who, with Glossie and Flossie, made up the ten who have traversed the world these hundreds of years with their generous master. They were all exceedingly beautiful, with slender limbs, spreading antlers, velvety dark eyes and smooth coats of fawn color spotted with white.

Claus loved them at once, and has loved them ever since, for they are loyal friends and have rendered him priceless service.

The new harness fitted them nicely and soon they were all fastened to the sledge by twos, with Glossie and Flossie in the lead. These wore the strings of sleigh-bells, and were so delighted with the music they made that they kept prancing up and down to make the bells ring.

Claus now seated himself in the sledge, drew

a warm robe over his knees and his fur cap over his ears, and cracked his long whip as a signal to start.

Instantly the ten leaped forward and were away like the wind, while jolly Claus laughed gleefully to see them run and shouted a song in his big, hearty voice:

"With a ho, ho, ho!
And a ha, ha, ha!
And a ho, ho, ha, ha, hee!
Now away we go
O'er the frozen snow,
As merry as we can be!
There are many joys
In our load of toys,
As many a child will know;
We'll scatter them wide
On our wild night ride
O'er the crisp and sparkling snow!"

Now it was on this same Christmas Eve that little Margot and her brother Dick and her cousins

Ned and Sara, who were visiting at Margot's house, came in from making a snow man, with their clothes damp, their mittens dripping and their shoes and stockings wet through and through. They were not scolded, for Margot's mother knew the snow was melting, but they were sent early to bed that their clothes might be hung over chairs to dry. The shoes were placed on the red tiles of the hearth, where the heat from the hot embers would strike them, and the stockings were carefully hung in a row by the chimney, directly over the fireplace. That was the reason Santa Claus noticed them when he came down the chimney that night and all the household were fast asleep. He was in a tremendous hurry and seeing the stockings all belonged to children he quickly stuffed his toys into them and dashed up the chimney again, appearing on the roof so suddenly that the reindeer were astonished at his agility.

"I wish they would all hang up their stockings," he thought, as he drove to the next chimney. "It would save me a lot of time and I could then visit more children before daybreak."

When Margot and Dick and Ned and Sara jumped out of bed next morning and ran downstairs to get their stockings from the fireplace they were filled with delight to find the toys from Santa Claus inside them. In fact, I think they found more presents in their stockings than any other children of that city had received, for Santa Claus was in a hurry and did not stop to count the toys.

Of course they told all their little friends about it, and of course every one of them decided to hang his own stockings by the fireplace the next Christmas Eve. Even Bessie Blithesome, who made a visit to that city with her father, the great Lord of Lerd, heard the story from the children and hung her own pretty stockings by the chimney when she returned home at Christmas time.

On his next trip Santa Claus found so many stockings hung up in anticipation of his visit that he could fill them in a jiffy and be away again in half the time required to hunt the children up and place the toys by their bedsides.

The custom grew year after year, and has

always been a great help to Santa Claus. And, with so many children to visit, he surely needs all the help we are able to give him.

12. The First Christmas Tree

Claus had always kept his promise to the Knooks by returning to the Laughing Valley by daybreak, but only the swiftness of his reindeer has enabled him to do this, for he travels over all the world.

He loved his work and he loved the brisk night ride on his sledge and the gay tinkle of the sleigh-bells. On that first trip with the ten reindeer only Glossie and Flossie wore bells; but each year thereafter for eight years Claus carried presents to the children of the Gnome King, and that good-natured monarch gave him in return a string of bells at each visit, so that finally every one of the ten deer was supplied, and you may imagine what a merry tune the bells played as the sledge sped over the snow.

The children's stockings were so long that it required a great many toys to fill them, and soon

Claus found there were other things besides toys that children love. So he sent some of the Fairies, who were always his good friends, into the Tropics, from whence they returned with great bags full of oranges and bananas which they had plucked from the trees. And other Fairies flew to the wonderful Valley of Phunnyland, where delicious candies and bonbons grow thickly on the bushes, and returned laden with many boxes of sweet-meats for the little ones. These things Santa Claus, on each Christmas Eve, placed in the long stockings, together with his toys, and the children were glad to get them, you may be sure.

There are also warm countries where there is no snow in winter, but Claus and his reindeer visited them as well as the colder climes, for there were little wheels inside the runners of his sledge which permitted it to run as smoothly over bare ground as on the snow. And the children who lived in the warm countries learned to know the name of Santa Claus as well as those who lived nearer to the Laughing Valley.

Once, just as the reindeer were ready to start

on their yearly trip, a Fairy came to Claus and told him of three little children who lived beneath a rude tent of skins on a broad plain where there were no trees whatever. These poor babies were miserable and unhappy, for their parents were ignorant people who neglected them sadly. Claus resolved to visit these children before he returned home, and during his ride he picked up the bushy top of a pine tree which the wind had broken off and placed it in his sledge.

It was nearly morning when the deer stopped before the lonely tent of skins where the poor children lay asleep. Claus at once planted the bit of pine tree in the sand and stuck many candles on the branches. Then he hung some of his prettiest toys on the tree, as well as several bags of candies. It did not take long to do all this, for Santa Claus works quickly, and when all was ready he lighted the candles and, thrusting his head in at the opening of the tent, he shouted: "Merry Christmas, little ones!"

With that he leaped into his sledge and was out of sight before the children, rubbing the sleep from their eyes, could come out to see who had called them.

You can imagine the wonder and joy of those little ones, who had never in their lives known a real pleasure before, when they saw the tree, sparkling with lights that shone brilliant in the gray dawn and hung with toys enough to make them happy for years to come! They joined hands and danced around the tree, shouting and laughing, until they were obliged to pause for breath. And their parents, also, came out to look and wonder, and thereafter had more respect and consideration for their children, since Santa Claus had honored them with such beautiful gifts.

The idea of the Christmas tree pleased Claus, and so the following year he carried many of them in his sledge and set them up in the homes of poor people who seldom saw trees, and placed candles and toys on the branches. Of course he could not carry enough trees in one load of all who wanted them, but in some homes the fathers were able to get trees and have them all ready for Santa Claus when he arrived; and these the good

Claus always decorated as prettily as possible and hung with toys enough for all the children who came to see the tree lighted.

These novel ideas and the generous manner in which they were carried out made the children long for that one night in the year when their friend Santa Claus should visit them, and as such anticipation is very pleasant and comforting the little ones gleaned much happiness by wondering what would happen when Santa Claus next arrived.

Perhaps you remember that stern Baron Braun who once drove Claus from his castle and forbade him to visit his children? Well, many years afterward, when the old Baron was dead and his son ruled in his place, the new Baron Braun came to the house of Claus with his train of knights and pages and henchmen and, dismounting from his charger, bared his head humbly before the friend of children.

"My father did not know your goodness and worth," he said, "and therefore threatened to hang you from the castle walls. But I have children of my own, who long for a visit from Santa Claus, and I have come to beg that you will favor them hereafter as you do other children."

Claus was pleased with this speech, for Castle Braun was the only place he had never visited, and he gladly promised to bring presents to the Baron's children the next Christmas Eve.

The Baron went away contented, and Claus kept his promise faithfully.

Thus did this man, through very goodness, conquer the hearts of all; and it is no wonder he was ever merry and gay, for there was no home in the wide world where he was not welcomed more royally than any king.

Old Age

1. The Mantle of Immortality

And now we come to a turning-point in the career of Santa Claus, and it is my duty to relate the most remarkable that has happened since the world began or mankind was created.

We have followed the life of Claus from the time he was found a helpless infant by the Wood-Nymph Necile and reared to manhood in the great Forest of Burzee. And we know how he began to make toys for children and how, with the assistance and goodwill of the immortals, he was able to distribute them to the little ones throughout the world.

For many years he carried on this noble work; for the simple, hard-working life he led gave him perfect health and strength. And doubtless a man can live longer in the beautiful Laughing Valley, where there are no cares and everything is peaceful and merry, than in any other part of the world.

But when many years had rolled away Santa Claus grew old. The long beard of golden brown that once covered his cheeks and chin gradually became gray, and finally turned to pure white. His hair was white, too, and there were wrinkles at the corners of his eyes, which showed plainly when he laughed. He had never been a very tall man, and now he became fat, and waddled very much like a duck when he walked. But in spite of these things he remained as lively as ever, and was just as jolly and gay, and his kind eyes sparkled as brightly as they did that first day when he came to the Laughing Valley.

Yet a time is sure to come when every mortal who has grown old and lived his life is required to leave this world for another; so it is no wonder that, after Santa Claus had driven his reindeer on many and many a Christmas Eve, those stanch friends finally whispered among themselves that they had probably drawn his sledge for the last time.

Then all the Forest of Burzee became sad and all the Laughing Valley was hushed; for every living thing that had known Claus had used to love him and to brighten at the sound of his footsteps or the notes of his merry whistle.

No doubt the old man's strength was at last exhausted, for he made no more toys, but lay on his bed as in a dream.

The Nymph Necile, she who had reared him and been his foster-mother, was still youthful and strong and beautiful, and it seemed to her but a short time since this aged, gray-bearded man had lain in her arms and smiled on her with his innocent, baby lips.

In this is shown the difference between mortals and immortals.

It was fortunate that the great Ak came to the Forest at this time. Necile sought him with troubled eyes and told him of the fate that threatened their friend Claus.

At once the Master became grave, and he leaned upon his ax and stroked his grizzled beard thoughtfully for many minutes. Then suddenly he stood up straight, and poised his powerful head with firm resolve, and stretched out his great right arm as if determined on doing some mighty deed. For a thought had come to him so grand in its conception that all the world might well bow before the Master Woodsman and honor his name forever!

It is well known that when the great Ak once undertakes to do a thing he never hesitates an instant. Now he summoned his fleetest messengers, and sent them in a flash to many parts of the earth. And when they were gone he turned to the anxious Necile and comforted her, saying: "Be of good heart, my child; our friend still lives. And now run to your Queen and tell her that I have summoned a council of all the immortals of the world to meet with me here in Burzee this night. If they obey, and harken unto my words, Claus will drive his reindeer for countless ages yet to come."

At midnight there was a wondrous scene in the ancient Forest of Burzee, where for the first time in many centuries the rulers of the immortals who inhabit the earth were gathered together.

There was the Queen of the Water Sprites, whose beautiful form was as clear as crystal but continually dripped water on the bank of moss where she sat. And beside her was the King of the Sleep Fays, who carried a wand from the end of which a fine dust fell all around, so that no mortal could keep awake long enough to see him, as mortal eyes were sure to close in sleep as soon as the dust filled them. And next to him sat the

Gnome King, whose people inhabit all that region under the earth's surface, where they guard the precious metals and the jewel stones that lie buried in rock and ore. At his right hand stood the King of the Sound Imps, who had wings on his feet, for his people are swift to carry all sounds that are made. When they are busy they carry the sounds but short distances, for there are many of them; but sometimes they speed with the sounds to places miles and miles away from where they are made. The King of the Sound Imps had an anxious and careworn face, for most people have no consideration for his Imps and, especially the boys and girls, make a great many unnecessary sounds which the Imps are obliged to carry when they might be better employed.

The next in the circle of immortals was the King of the Wind Demons, slender of frame, restless and uneasy at being confined to one place for even an hour. Once in a while he would leave his place and circle around the glade, and each time he did this the Fairy Queen was obliged to untangle the flowing locks of her golden hair and tuck them back of her pink ears. But she did not complain, for it was not often that the King of the Wind Demons came into the heart of the Forest. After the Fairy Queen, whose home you know was in old Burzee, came the King of the Light Elves, with his two Princes, Flash and Twilight, at his back. He never went anywhere without his Princes, for they were so mischievous that he dared not let them wander alone.

Prince Flash bore a lightning-bolt in his right hand and a horn of gunpowder in his left, and his bright eyes roved constantly around, as if he longed to use his blinding flashes. Prince Twilight held a great snuffer in one hand and a big black cloak in the other, and it is well known that unless Twilight is carefully watched the snuffers or the cloak will throw everything into darkness, and Darkness is the greatest enemy the King of the Light Elves has.

In addition to the immortals I have named were the King of the Knooks, who had come from his home in the jungles of India; and the King of the Ryls, who lived among the gay flowers and luscious fruits of Valencia. Sweet Queen Zurline of the Wood-Nymphs completed the circle of immortals.

But in the center of the circle sat three others who possessed powers so great that all the Kings and Queens showed them reverence.

These were Ak, the Master Woodsman of the World, who rules the forests and the orchards and the groves; and Kern, the Master Husbandman of the World, who rules the grain fields and the meadows and the gardens; and Bo, the Master Mariner of the World, who rules the seas and all the craft that float thereon. And all other immortals are more or less subject to these three.

When all had assembled the Master Woodsman of the World stood up to address them, since he himself had summoned them to the council.

Very clearly he told them the story of Claus, beginning at the time when as a babe he had been adopted a child of the Forest, and telling of his noble and generous nature and his life-long labors to make children happy.

"And now," said Ak, "when he had won the

love of all the world, the Spirit of Death is hovering over him. Of all men who have inhabited the earth none other so well deserves immortality, for such a life cannot be spared so long as there are children of mankind to miss him and to grieve over his loss. We immortals are the servants of the world, and to serve the world we were permitted in the Beginning to exist. But what one of us is more worthy of immortality than this man Claus, who so sweetly ministers to the little children?"

He paused and glanced around the circle, to find every immortal listening to him eagerly and nodding approval. Finally the King of the Wind Demons, who had been whistling softly to himself, cried out: "What is your desire, O Ak?"

"To bestow upon Claus the Mantle of Immortality!" said Ak, boldly.

That this demand was wholly unexpected was proved by the immortals springing to their feet and looking into each other's face with dismay and then upon Ak with wonder. For it was a grave matter, this parting with the Mantle of Immortality.

The Queen of the Water Sprites spoke in her low, clear voice, and the words sounded like raindrops splashing upon a window-pane.

"In all the world there is but one Mantle of Immortality," she said.

The King of the Sound Fays added: "It has existed since the Beginning, and no mortal has ever dared to claim it."

And the Master Mariner of the World arose and stretched his limbs, saying: "Only by the vote of every immortal can it be bestowed upon a mortal."

"I know all this," answered Ak, quietly. "But the Mantle exists, and if it was created, as you say, in the Beginning, it was because the Supreme Master knew that some day it would be required. Until now no mortal has deserved it, but who among you dares deny that the good Claus deserves it? Will you not all vote to bestow it upon him?"

They were silent, still looking upon one another questioningly.

"Of what use is the Mantle of Immortality

unless it is worn?" demanded Ak. "What will it profit any one of us to allow it to remain in its lonely shrine for all time to come?"

"Enough!" cried the Gnome King, abruptly. "We will vote on the matter, yes or no. For my part, I say yes!"

"And I!" said the Fairy Queen, promptly, and Ak rewarded her with a smile.

"My people in Burzee tell me they have learned to love him; therefore I vote to give Claus the Mantle," said the King of the Ryls.

"He is already a comrade of the Knooks," announced the ancient King of that band. "Let him have immortality!"

"Let him have it—let him have it!" sighed the King of the Wind Demons.

"Why not?" asked the King of the Sleep Fays. "He never disturbs the slumbers my people allow humanity. Let the good Claus be immortal!"

"I do not object," said the King of the Sound Imps.

"Nor I," murmured the Queen of the Water Sprites.

"If Claus does not receive the Mantle it is clear none other can ever claim it," remarked the King of the Light Elves, "so let us have done with the thing for all time."

"The Wood-Nymphs were first to adopt him," said Queen Zurline. "Of course I shall vote to make him immortal."

Ak now turned to the Master Husbandman of the World, who held up his right arm and said, "Yes!"

And the Master Mariner of the World did likewise, after which Ak, with sparkling eyes and smiling face, cried out: "I thank you, fellow immortals! For all have voted 'yes,' and so to our dear Claus shall fall the one Mantle of Immortality that it is in our power to bestow!"

"Let us fetch it at once," said the Fay King; "I'm in a hurry."

They bowed assent, and instantly the Forest glade was deserted. But in a place midway between the earth and the sky was suspended a gleaming crypt of gold and platinum, aglow with soft lights shed from the facets of countless gems.

Within a high dome hung the precious Mantle of Immortality, and each immortal placed a hand on the hem of the splendid Robe and said, as with one voice: "We bestow this Mantle upon Claus, who is called the Patron Saint of Children!"

At this the Mantle came away from its lofty crypt, and they carried it to the house in the Laughing Valley.

The Spirit of Death was crouching very near to the bedside of Claus, and as the immortals approached she sprang up and motioned them back with an angry gesture. But when her eyes fell upon the Mantle they bore she shrank away with a low moan of disappointment and quitted that house forever.

Softly and silently the immortal Band dropped upon Claus the precious Mantle, and it closed about him and sank into the outlines of his body and disappeared from view. It became a part of his being, and neither mortal nor immortal might ever take it from him.

Then the Kings and Queens who had wrought this great deed dispersed to their various homes, and all were well contented that they had added another immortal to their Band.

And Claus slept on, the red blood of everlasting life coursing swiftly through his veins; and on his brow was a tiny drop of water that had fallen from the ever-melting gown of the Queen of the Water Sprites, and over his lips hovered a tender kiss that had been left by the sweet Nymph Necile. For she had stolen in when the others were gone to gaze with rapture upon the immortal form of her foster son.

2. When the World Grew Old

The next morning, when Santa Claus opened his eyes and gazed around the familiar room, which he had feared he might never see again, he was astonished to find his old strength renewed and to feel the red blood of perfect health coursing through his veins. He sprang from his bed and stood where the bright sunshine came in through his window and flooded him with its merry, dancing rays. He did not then understand what had happened to restore to him the vigor of youth, but in spite of the fact that his beard remained the color of snow and that wrinkles still lingered in the corners of his bright eyes, old Santa Claus felt as brisk and merry as a boy of sixteen, and was soon whistling contentedly as he busied himself fashioning new toys.

Then Ak came to him and told of the Mantle of Immortality and how Claus had won it through his love for little children.

It made old Santa look grave for a moment to think he had been so favored; but it also made him glad to realize that now he need never fear being parted from his dear ones. At once he began preparations for making a remarkable assortment of pretty and amusing playthings, and in larger quantities than ever before; for now that he might always devote himself to this work he decided that no child in the world, poor or rich, should hereafter go without a Christmas gift if he could manage to supply it.

The world was new in the days when dear old Santa Claus first began toy-making and won, by his loving deeds, the Mantle of Immortality. And the task of supplying cheering words, sympathy and pretty playthings to all the young of his race did not seem a difficult undertaking at all. But every year more and more children were born into the world, and these, when they grew up, began spreading slowly over all the face of the earth, seeking new homes; so that Santa Claus found each year that his journeys must extend farther and farther from the Laughing Valley, and that the packs of toys must be made larger and ever larger.

So at length he took counsel with his fellow immortals how his work might keep pace with the increasing number of children that none might be neglected. And the immortals were so greatly interested in his labors that they gladly rendered him their assistance. Ak gave him his man Kilter, "the silent and swift." And the Knook Prince gave him Peter, who was more crooked and less surly than any of his brothers. And the Ryl Prince gave him Nuter, the sweetest tempered Ryl ever known. And the Fairy Queen gave him Wisk, that tiny, mischievous but lovable Fairy who knows today almost as many children as does Santa Claus himself.

With these people to help make the toys and to keep his house in order and to look after the sledge and the harness, Santa Claus found it much easier to prepare his yearly load of gifts, and his days began to follow one another smoothly and pleasantly.

Yet after a few generations his worries were renewed, for it was remarkable how the number of people continued to grow, and how many more children there were every year to be served. When the people filled all the cities and lands of one country they wandered into another part of the world; and the men cut down the trees in many of the great forests that had been ruled by Ak, and with the wood they built new cities, and where the forests had been were fields of grain and herds of browsing cattle.

You might think the Master Woodsman would rebel at the loss of his forests; but not so. The wisdom of Ak was mighty and farseeing.

"The world was made for men," said he to Santa Claus, "and I have but guarded the forests until men needed them for their use. I am glad my strong trees can furnish shelter for men's weak bodies, and warm them through the cold winters. But I hope they will not cut down all the trees, for mankind needs the shelter of the woods in summer as much as the warmth of blazing logs in winter. And, however crowded the world may grow, I do not think men will ever come to Burzee, nor to the Great Black Forest, nor to the wooded wilderness of Braz; unless they seek their shades for pleasure and not to destroy their giant trees."

By and by people made ships from the tree trunks and crossed over oceans and built cities in far lands; but the oceans made little difference to the journeys of Santa Claus. His reindeer sped over the waters as swiftly as over land, and his sledge headed from east to west and followed in the wake of the sun. So that as the earth rolled slowly over Santa Claus had all of twenty-four hours to encircle it each Christmas Eve, and the speedy reindeer enjoyed these wonderful journeys more and more.

So year after year, and generation after generation, and century after century, the world grew older and the people became more numerous and the labors of Santa Claus steadily increased. The fame of his good deeds spread to every household where children dwelt. And all the little ones loved him dearly; and the fathers and mothers honored him for the happiness he had given them when they too were young; and the aged grandsires and granddames remembered him with tender gratitude and blessed his name.

3. The Deputies of Santa Claus

However, there was one evil following in the path of civilization that caused Santa Claus a vast amount of trouble before he discovered a way to overcome it. But, fortunately, it was the last trial he was forced to undergo.

One Christmas Eve, when his reindeer had leaped to the top of a new building, Santa Claus was surprised to find that the chimney had been built much smaller than usual. But he had no time to think about it just then, so he drew in his breath and made himself as small as possible and slid down the chimney.

"I ought to be at the bottom by this time," he thought, as he continued to slip downward; but no fireplace of any sort met his view, and by and by he reached the very end of the chimney, which was in the cellar.

"This is odd!" he reflected, much puzzled by this experience. "If there is no fireplace, what on earth is the chimney good for?"

Then he began to climb out again, and found it hard work—the space being so small. And on his way up he noticed a thin, round pipe sticking through the side of the chimney, but could not guess what it was for.

Finally he reached the roof and said to the reindeer: "There was no need of my going down that chimney, for I could find no fireplace through which to enter the house. I fear the children who live there must go without playthings this Christmas."

Then he drove on, but soon came to another new house with a small chimney. This caused Santa Claus to shake his head doubtfully, but he tried the chimney, nevertheless, and found it exactly like the other. Moreover, he nearly stuck fast in the narrow flue and tore his jacket trying to get out again; so, although he came to several such chimneys that night, he did not venture to descend any more of them.

"What in the world are people thinking of, to build such useless chimneys?" he exclaimed. "In all the years I have traveled with my reindeer I have never seen the like before."

True enough; but Santa Claus had not then discovered that stoves had been invented and were fast coming into use. When he did find it out he wondered how the builders of those houses could have so little consideration for him, when they knew very well it was his custom to climb down chimneys and enter houses by way of the fireplaces. Perhaps the men who built those houses had outgrown their own love for toys, and were indifferent whether Santa Claus called on their children or not. Whatever the explanation might be, the poor children were forced to bear the burden of grief and disappointment.

The following year Santa Claus found more and more of the new-fashioned chimneys that had no fireplaces, and the next year still more. The third year, so numerous had the narrow chimneys become, he even had a few toys left in his sledge that he was unable to give away, because he could not get to the children.

The matter had now become so serious that it worried the good man greatly, and he decided to talk it over with Kilter and Peter and Nuter and Wisk.

Kilter already knew something about it, for it had been his duty to run around to all the houses, just before Christmas, and gather up the notes and letters to Santa Claus that the children had written, telling what they wished put in their stockings or hung on their Christmas trees. But Kilter was a silent fellow, and seldom spoke of what he saw in the cities and villages. The others were very indignant.

"Those people act as if they do not wish their children to be made happy!" said sensible Peter, in a vexed tone. "The idea of shutting out such a generous friend to their little ones!"

"But it is my intention to make children happy

whether their parents wish it or not," returned Santa Claus. "Years ago, when I first began making toys, children were even more neglected by their parents than they are now; so I have learned to pay no attention to thoughtless or selfish parents, but to consider only the longings of childhood."

"You are right, my master," said Nuter, the Ryl. "Many children would lack a friend if you did not consider them, and try to make them happy."

"Then," declared the laughing Wisk, "we must abandon any thought of using these new-fashioned chimneys, but become burglars, and break into the houses some other way."

"What way?" asked Santa Claus.

"Why, walls of brick and wood and plaster are nothing to Fairies. I can easily pass through them whenever I wish, and so can Peter and Nuter and Kilter. Is it not so, comrades?"

"I often pass through the walls when I gather up the letters," said Kilter, and that was a long speech for him, and so surprised Peter and Nuter that their big round eyes nearly popped out of their heads.

"Therefore," continued the Fairy, "you may as well take us with you on your next journey, and when we come to one of those houses with stoves instead of fireplaces we will distribute the toys to the children without the need of using a chimney."

"That seems to me a good plan," replied Santa Claus, well pleased at having solved the problem. "We will try it next year."

That was how the Fairy, the Pixie, the Knook and the Ryl all rode in the sledge with their master the following Christmas Eve; and they had no trouble at all in entering the new-fashioned houses and leaving toys for the children that lived in them.

And their deft services not only relieved Santa Claus of much labor, but enabled him to complete his own work more quickly than usual, so that the merry party found themselves at home with an empty sledge a full hour before daybreak.

The only drawback to the journey was that the mischievous Wisk persisted in tickling the reindeer with a long feather, to see them jump; and Santa Claus found it necessary to watch him every minute and to tweak his long ears once or twice to make him behave himself.

But, taken all together, the trip was a great success, and to this day the four little folk always accompany Santa Claus on his yearly ride and help him in the distribution of his gifts.

But the indifference of parents, which had so annoyed the good Saint, did not continue very long, and Santa Claus soon found they were really anxious he should visit their homes on Christmas Eve and leave presents for their children.

So, to lighten his task, which was fast becoming very difficult indeed, old Santa decided to ask the parents to assist him.

"Get your Christmas trees all ready for my coming," he said to them; "and then I shall be able to leave the presents without loss of time, and you can put them on the trees when I am gone."

And to others he said: "See that the children's stockings are hung up in readiness for my coming, and then I can fill them as quick as a wink."

And often, when parents were kind and good-natured, Santa Claus would simply fling down his package of gifts and leave the fathers and mothers to fill the stockings after he had darted away in his sledge.

"I will make all loving parents my deputies!" cried the jolly old fellow. "And they shall help me do my work. For in this way I shall save many precious minutes and few children need be neglected for lack of time to visit them."

Besides carrying around the big packs in his swift-flying sledge old Santa began to send great heaps of toys to the toy-shops, so that if parents wanted larger supplies for their children they could easily get them; and if any children were, by chance, missed by Santa Claus on his yearly rounds, they could go to the toy-shops and get enough to make them happy and contented. For the loving friend of the little ones decided that no child, if he could help it, should long for toys in vain. And the toy-shops also proved convenient whenever a child fell ill, and needed a new toy to amuse it; and sometimes, on birthdays, the fathers and mothers go to the toy-shops and get pretty gifts for their children in honor of the happy event.

Perhaps you will now understand how, in spite of the bigness of the world, Santa Claus is able to supply all the children with beautiful gifts. To be sure, the old gentleman is rarely seen in these days; but it is not because he tries to keep out of sight, I assure you. Santa Claus is the same loving friend of children that in the old days used to play and romp with them by the hour; and I know he would love to do the same now, if he had the time. But, you see, he is so busy all the year making toys, and so hurried on that one night when he visits our homes with his packs, that he comes and goes among us like a flash; and it is almost impossible to catch a glimpse of him.

And, although there are millions and millions more children in the world than there used to be, Santa Claus has never been known to complain of their increasing numbers.

"The more the merrier!" he cries, with his jolly laugh; and the only difference to him is the fact that his little workmen have to make their busy fingers fly faster every year to satisfy the demands of so many little ones.

"In all this world there is nothing so beautiful as a happy child," says good old Santa Claus; and if he had his way the children would all be beautiful, for all would be happy.

LOUISA MAY ALCOTT

1832-1888

A CHRISTMAS TURKEY, AND HOW IT CAME

I know we couldn't do it."

"I say we could, if we all helped."

"How can we?"

"I've planned lots of ways; only you mustn't laugh at them, and you mustn't say a word to mother. I want it to be all a surprise."

"She'll find us out."

"No, she won't, if we tell her we won't get into mischief."

"Fire away, then, and let's hear your fine plans."

"We must talk softly, or we shall wake father. He's got a headache."

A curious change came over the faces of the two boys as their sister lowered her voice, with a nod toward a half-opened door. They looked sad and ashamed, and Kitty sighed as she spoke, for all knew that father's headaches always began by his coming home stupid or cross, with only a part of his wages; and mother always cried when she thought they did not see her, and after the long sleep father looked as if he didn't like to meet their eyes, but went off early.

They knew what it meant, but never spoke of it—only pondered over it, and mourned with mother at the change which was slowly altering their kind industrious father into a moody man, and mother into an anxious over-worked woman.

Kitty was thirteen, and a very capable girl, who helped with the housekeeping, took care of the two little ones, and went to school. Tommy and Sammy looked up to her and thought her a remarkably good sister. Now, as they sat round the stove having "a go-to-bed warm," the three heads were close together; and the boys listened eagerly to Kitty's plans, while the rattle of the sewing-machine in another room went on as tirelessly as it had done all day, for mother's work was more and more needed every month.

"Well!" began Kitty, in an impressive tone, "we all know that there won't be a bit of Christmas in this family if we don't make it. Mother's too busy, and father don't care, so we must see what we can do; for I should be mortified to death to go to school and say I hadn't had any turkey or plum-pudding. Don't expect presents; but we *must* have some kind of a decent dinner."

"So I say; I'm tired of fish and potatoes," said Sammy, the younger.

"But where's the dinner coming from?" asked Tommy, who had already taken some of the cares of life on his young shoulders, and knew that Christmas dinners did not walk into people's houses without money.

"We'll earn it"; and Kitty looked like a small Napoleon planning the passage of the Alps. "You, Tom, must go early to-morrow to Mr. Brisket and offer to carry baskets. He will be dreadfully busy, and want you, I know; and you are so strong you can lug as much as some of the big fellows. He pays well, and if he won't give much money, you can take your wages in things to eat. We want everything."

"What shall I do?" cried Sammy, while Tom sat turning this plan over in his mind.

"Take the old shovel and clear sidewalks. The snow came on purpose to help you."

"It's awful hard work, and the shovel's half gone," began Sammy, who preferred to spend his holiday coasting on an old tea-tray.

"Don't growl, or you won't get any dinner," said Tom, making up his mind to lug baskets for the good of the family, like a manly lad as he was.

"I," continued Kitty, "have taken the hardest part of all; for after my work is done, and the babies safely settled, I'm going to beg for the leavings of the holly and pine swept out of the church down below, and make some wreaths and sell them."

"If you can," put in Tommy, who had tried pencils, and failed to make a fortune.

"Not in the street?" cried Sam, looking alarmed.

"Yes, at the corner of the Park. I'm bound to make some money, and don't see any other way. I shall put on an old hood and shawl, and no one will know me. Don't care if they do." And Kitty tried to mean what she said, but in her heart she felt that it would be a trial to her pride if any of her schoolmates should happen to recognize her.

"Don't believe you'll do it."

"See if I don't; for I *will* have a good dinner one day in the year."

"Well, it doesn't seem right for us to do it. Father ought to take care of us, and we only buy some presents with the little bit we earn. He never gives us anything now." And Tommy scowled at the bedroom door, with a strong sense of injury struggling with affection in his boyish heart.

"Hush!" cried Kitty. "Don't blame him. Mother says we never must forget he's our father. I try not to; but when she cries, it's hard to feel as I ought." And a sob made the little girl stop short as she poked the fire to hide the trouble in the face that should have been all smiles.

For a moment the room was very still, as the snow beat on the window, and the fire-light flickered over the six shabby little boots put up on the stove hearth to dry.

Tommy's cheerful voice broke the silence, saying stoutly, "Well, if I've got to work all day, I guess I'll go to bed early. Don't fret, Kit. We'll help all we can, and have a good time; see if we don't."

"I'll go out real early, and shovel like fury. Maybe I'll get a dollar. Would that buy a turkey?" asked Sammy, with the air of a millionaire.

"No, dear; one big enough for us would cost two, I'm afraid. Perhaps we'll have one sent us. We belong to the church, though folks don't know how poor we are now, and we can't beg." And Kitty bustled about, clearing up, rather exercised in her mind about going and asking for the much-desired fowl.

Soon all three were fast asleep, and nothing but the whir of the machine broke the quiet that fell upon the house. Then from the inner room a man came and sat over the fire with his head in his hands and his eyes fixed on the ragged little boots left to dry. He had heard the children's talk; and his heart was very heavy as he looked about the shabby room that used to be so neat and pleasant. What he thought no one knows, what he did we shall see by-and-by; but the sorrow and shame and tender silence of his children worked a miracle that night more lasting and lovely than the white beauty which the snow wrought upon the sleeping city.

Bright and early the boys were away to their work; while Kitty sang as she dressed the little sisters, put the house in order, and made her mother smile at the mysterious hints she gave of something splendid which was going to happen. Father was gone, and though all rather dreaded evening, nothing was said; but each worked with a will, feeling that Christmas should be merry in spite of poverty and care.

All day Tommy lugged fat turkeys, roasts of beef, and every sort of vegetable for other people's good dinners on the morrow, wondering meanwhile where his own was coming from. Mr. Brisket had an army of boys trudging here and there, and was too busy to notice any particular lad till the hurry was over, and only a few belated buyers remained to be served. It was late; but the stores kept open, and though so tired he could hardly stand, brave Tommy held on when the other boys left, hoping to earn a trifle more by extra work. He sat down on a barrel to rest during a leisure moment, and presently his weary head nodded sideways into a basket of cranberries, where he slept quietly till the sound of gruff voices roused him.

It was Mr. Brisket scolding because one dinner had been forgotten.

"I told that rascal Beals to be sure and carry it, for the old gentleman will be in a rage if it doesn't come, and take away his custom. Every boy gone, and I can't leave the store, nor you either, Pat, with all the clearing up to do."

"Here's a by, sir, slapin illigant forninst the cranberries, bad luck to him!" answered Pat, with a shake that set poor Tom on his legs, wide awake at once.

"*Good* luck to him, you mean. Here, What's-your-name, you take this basket to that number, and I'll make it worth your while," said Mr. Brisket, much relieved by this unexpected help.

"All right, sir"; and Tommy trudged off as briskly as his tired legs would let him, cheering the long cold walk with visions of the turkey with which his employer might reward him, for there were piles of them, and Pat was to have one for his family.

His brilliant dreams were disappointed, however, for Mr. Brisket naturally supposed Tom's father would attend to that part of the dinner, and generously heaped a basket with vegetables, rosy apples, and a quart of cranberries.

"There, if you ain't too tired, you can take one more load to that number, and a merry Christmas to you!" said the stout man, handing over his gift with the promised dollar.

"Thank you, sir; good-night," answered Tom, shouldering his last load with a grateful smile, and trying not to look longingly at the poultry; for he had set his heart on at least a skinny bird as a surprise to Kit.

Sammy's adventures that day had been more varied and his efforts more successful, as we shall see, in the end, for Sammy was a most engaging little fellow, and no one could look into his blue eyes without wanting to pat his curly yellow head with one hand while the other gave him something. The cares of life had not lessened his confidence in people; and only the most abandoned ruffians had the heart to deceive or disappoint him. His very tribulations usually led to something pleasant, and whatever happened, sunshiny Sam came right side up, lucky and laughing.

Undaunted by the drifts or the cold wind, he marched off with the remains of the old shovel to seek his fortune, and found it at the third house where he called. The first two sidewalks were easy jobs; and he pocketed his ninepences with a growing conviction that this was his chosen work. The third sidewalk was a fine long one, for the house stood on the corner, and two pavements must be cleared.

"It ought to be fifty cents; but perhaps they won't give me so much, I'm such a young one. I'll show 'em I can work, though, like a man"; and Sammy rang the bell with the energy of a telegraph boy.

Before the bell could be answered, a big boy rushed up, exclaiming roughly, "Get out of this!

I'm going to have the job. You can't do it. Start, now, or I'll chuck you into a snow-bank."

"I won't!" answered Sammy, indignant at the brutal tone and unjust claim. "I got here first, and it's my job. You let me alone. I ain't afraid of you or your snow-banks either."

The big boy wasted no time in words, for steps were heard inside, but after a brief scuffle hauled Sammy, fighting bravely all the way, down the steps, and tumbled him into a deep drift. Then he ran up the steps, and respectfully asked for the job when a neat maid opened the door. He would have got it if Sam had not roared out, as he floundered in the drift, "I came first. He knocked me down 'cause I'm the smallest. Please let me do it; please!"

Before another word could be said, a little old lady appeared in the hall, trying to look stern, and failing entirely, because she was the picture of a dear fat, cosey grandma.

"Send that *bad* big boy away, Maria, and call in the poor little fellow. I saw the whole thing, and *he* shall have the job if he can do it."

The bully slunk away, and Sammy came panting up the steps, white with snow, a great bruise on his forehead, and a beaming smile on his face, looking so like a jolly little Santa Claus who had taken a "header" out of his sleigh that the maid laughed, and the old lady exclaimed, "Bless the boy! He's dreadfully hurt, and doesn't know it. Come in and be brushed and get your breath, child, and tell me how that scamp came to treat you so."

Nothing loath to be comforted, Sammy told his little tale while Maria dusted him off on the mat, and the old lady hovered in the doorway of the dining-room, where a nice breakfast smoked and smelled so deliciously that the boy sniffed the odor of coffee and buckwheats like a hungry hound.

"He'll get his death if he goes to work till he's dried a bit. Put him over the register, Maria, and I'll give him a hot drink, for it's bitter cold, poor dear!"

Away trotted the kind old lady, and in a minute came back with coffee and cakes, on which Sammy feasted as he warmed his toes and told Kitty's plans for Christmas, led on by the old lady's questions, and quite unconscious that he was letting all sorts of cats out of the bag.

Mrs. Bryant understood the little story, and made her plans also, for the rosy-faced boy was very like a little grandson who died last year, and her sad old heart was very tender to all other small boys. So she found out where Sammy lived, and nodded and smiled at him most cheerily as he tugged stoutly away at the snow on the long pavements till all was done, and the little workman came for his wages.

A bright silver dollar and a pocketful of gingerbread sent him off a rich and happy boy to shovel and sweep till noon, when he proudly showed his earnings at home, and feasted the babies on the carefully hoarded cake, for Dilly and Dot were the idols of the household.

"Now, Sammy dear, I want you to take my place here this afternoon, for mother will have to take her work home by-and-by, and I must sell my wreaths. I only got enough green for six, and two bunches of holly; but if I can sell them for ten or twelve cents apiece, I shall be glad. Girls never *can* earn as much money as boys somehow," sighed Kitty, surveying the thin wreaths tied up with carpet ravellings, and vainly puzzling her young wits over a sad problem.

"I'll give you some of my money if you don't get a dollar; then we'll be even. Men always take care of women, you know, and ought to," cried Sammy, setting a fine example to his father, if he had only been there to profit by it.

With thanks Kitty left him to rest on the old sofa, while the happy babies swarmed over him; and putting on the shabby hood and shawl, she slipped away to stand at the Park gate, modestly offering her little wares to the passers-by. A nice old gentleman bought two, and his wife scolded him for getting such bad ones; but the money gave more happiness than any other he spent that day. A child took a ten-cent bunch of holly with its red berries, and there Kitty's market ended. It was very cold, people were in a hurry, bolder hucksters pressed before the timid little girl, and the balloon man told her to "clear out."

Hoping for better luck, she tried several other

places; but the short afternoon was soon over, the streets began to thin, the keen wind chilled her to the bone, and her heart was very heavy to think that in all the rich, merry city, where Christmas gifts passed her in every hand, there were none for the dear babies and boys at home, and the Christmas dinner was a failure.

"I must go and get supper anyway; and I'll hang these up in our own rooms, as I can't sell them," said Kitty, wiping a very big tear from her cold cheek, and turning to go away.

A smaller, shabbier girl than herself stood near, looking at the bunch of holly with wistful eyes; and glad to do to others as she wished someone would do to her, Kitty offered the only thing she had to give, saying kindly, "You may have it; merry Christmas!" and ran away before the delighted child could thank her.

I am very sure that one of the spirits who fly about at this season of the year saw the little act, made a note of it, and in about fifteen minutes rewarded Kitty for her sweet remembrance of the golden rule.

As she went sadly homeward she looked up at some of the big houses where every window shone with the festivities of Christmas Eve, and more than one tear fell, for the little girl found life pretty hard just then.

"There don't seem to be any wreaths at these windows; perhaps they'd buy mine. I can't bear to go home with so little for my share," she said, stopping before one of the biggest and brightest of these fairy palaces, where the sound of music was heard, and many little heads peeped from behind the curtains as if watching for some one.

Kitty was just going up the steps to make another trial, when two small boys came racing round the corner, slipped on the icy pavement, and both went down with a crash that would have broken older bones. One was up in a minute, laughing; the other lay squirming and howling, "Oh, my knee! my knee!" till Kitty ran and picked him up with the motherly consolations she had learned to give.

"It's broken; I know it is," wailed the small sufferer as Kitty carried him up the steps, while his friend wildly rang the doorbell.

It was like going into fairy-land, for the house was all astir with a children's Christmas party. Servants flew about with smiling faces; open doors gave ravishing glimpses of a feast in one room and a splendid tree in another; while a crowd of little faces peered over the balusters in the hall above, eager to come down and enjoy the glories prepared for them.

A pretty young girl came to meet Kitty, and listened to her story of the accident, which proved to be less severe than it at first appeared; for Bertie, the injured party, forgot his anguish at sight of the tree, and hopped upstairs so nimbly that every one laughed.

"He said his leg was broken, but I guess he's all right," said Kitty, reluctantly turning from this happy scene to go out into the night again.

"Would you like to see our tree before the children come down?" asked the pretty girl, seeing the wistful look in the child's eyes, and the shine of half-dried tears on her cheek.

"Oh, yes; I never saw anything so lovely. I'd like to tell the babies all about it"; and Kitty's face beamed at the prospect, as if the kind words had melted all the frost away.

"How many babies are there?" asked the pretty girl, as she led the way into the brilliant room. Kitty told her, adding several other facts, for the friendly atmosphere seemed to make them friends at once.

"I will buy the wreaths, for we haven't any," said the girl in silk, as Kitty told how she was just coming to offer them when the boys fell.

It was pretty to see how carefully the little hostess laid away the shabby garlands and slipped a half-dollar into Kitty's hand; prettier still, to watch the sly way in which she tucked some bonbons, a red ball, a blue whip, two china dolls, two pairs of little mittens, and some gilded nuts into an empty box for "the babies"; and prettiest of all, to see the smiles and tears make April in Kitty's face as she tried to tell her thanks for this beautiful surprise.

The world was all right when she got into the street again and ran home with the precious box hugged close, feeling that at last she had something to make a merry Christmas of.

Shrieks of joy greeted her, for Sammy's nice old lady had sent a basket full of pies, nuts and raisins, oranges and cake, and—oh, happy Sammy!—a sled, all for love of the blue eyes that twinkled so merrily when he told her about the tea-tray. Piled upon this red car of triumph, Dilly and Dot were being dragged about, while the other treasures were set forth on the table.

"I must show mine," cried Kitty; "we'll look at them to-night, and have them to-morrow"; and amid more cries of rapture *her* box was unpacked, *her* money added to the pile in the middle of the table, where Sammy had laid his handsome contribution toward the turkey.

Before the story of the splendid tree was over, in came Tommy with his substantial offering and his hard-earned dollar.

"I'm afraid I ought to keep my money for shoes. I've walked the soles off these to-day, and can't go to school barefooted," he said, bravely trying to put the temptation of skates behind him.

"We've got a good dinner without a turkey, and perhaps we'd better not get it," added Kitty, with a sigh, as she surveyed the table, and remembered the blue knit hood marked seventy-five cents that she saw in a shop-window.

"Oh, we *must* have a turkey! We worked so hard for it, and it's so Christmasy," cried Sam, who always felt that pleasant things ought to happen.

"Must have turty," echoed the babies, as they eyed the dolls tenderly.

"You *shall* have a turkey, and there he is," said an unexpected voice, as a noble bird fell upon the table, and lay there kicking up his legs as if enjoying the surprise immensely.

It was father's voice, and there stood father, neither cross nor stupid, but looking as he used to look, kind and happy, and beside him was mother, smiling as they had not seen her smile for months. It was not because the work was well paid for, and more promised, but because she had received a gift that made the world bright, a home happy again— father's promise to drink no more.

"I've been working to-day as well as you, and you may keep your money for yourselves. There are shoes for all; and never again, please God, shall my children be ashamed of me, or want a dinner Christmas Day."

As father said this with a choke in his voice, and mother's head went down on his shoulder to hide the happy tears that wet her cheeks, the children didn't know whether to laugh or cry, till Kitty, with the instinct of a loving heart, settled the question by saying, as she held out her hands, "We haven't any tree, so let's dance around our goodies and be merry."

Then the tired feet in the old shoes forgot their weariness, and five happy little souls skipped gayly round the table, where, in the midst of all the treasures earned and given, father's Christmas turkey proudly lay in state.

WHAT THE BELLS
SAW AND SAID

B ells ring others to church, but go not in themselves."

No one saw the spirits of the bells up there in the old steeple at midnight on Christmas Eve. Six quaint figures, each wrapped in a shadowy cloak and wearing a bell-shaped cap. All were gray-headed, for they were among the oldest bell-spirits of the city, and "the light of other days" shone in their thoughtful eyes. Silently they sat, looking down on the snow-covered roofs glittering in the moonlight, and the quiet streets deserted by all but the watchmen on their chilly rounds, and such poor souls as wandered shelterless in the winter night. Presently one of the spirits said, in a tone, which, low as it was, filled the belfry with rever-berating echoes,—

"Well, brothers, are your reports ready of the year that now lies dying?"

All bowed their heads, and one of the oldest answered in a sonorous voice:—

"My report isn't all I could wish. You know I look down on the commercial part of our city and have fine opportunities for seeing what goes on there. It's my business to watch the business men, and upon my word I'm heartily ashamed of them sometimes. During the war they did nobly, giving their time and money, their sons and selves to the good cause, and I was proud of them. But now too many of them have fallen back into the old ways, and their motto seems to be, 'Every one for himself, and the devil take the hindmost.' Cheating, lying and stealing are hard words, and I don't mean to apply them to *all* who swarm about below there like ants on an ant-hill—*they* have other names for these things, but I'm old-fashioned and use plain words. There's a deal too much dishonesty in the world, and business seems to have become a game of hazard in which luck, not labor, wins the prize. When I was young, men were years making moderate fortunes, and were satisfied with them. They built them on sure foundations, knew how to enjoy them while they lived, and to leave a good name behind them when they died.

"Now it's anything for money; health, happiness, honor, life itself, are flung down on that great gaming-table, and they forget everything else in the excitement of success or the desperation of defeat. Nobody seems satisfied either, for those who win have little time or taste to enjoy their prosperity, and those who lose have little courage or patience to support them in adversity. They don't even fail as they used to. In my day when a merchant found himself embarrassed he didn't ruin others in order to save himself, but honestly confessed the truth, gave up everything, and began again. But now-a-days after all manner of dishonorable shifts there comes a grand crash; many suffer, but by some hocus-pocus the merchant saves enough to retire upon and live comfortably here or abroad. It's very evident that honor and honesty don't mean now what they used to mean in the days of old May, Higginson and Lawrence.

"They preach below here, and very well too

sometimes, for I often slide down the rope to peep and listen during service. But, bless you! they don't seem to lay either sermon, psalm or prayer to heart, for while the minister is doing his best, the congregation, tired with the breathless hurry of the week, sleep peacefully, calculate their chances for the morrow, or wonder which of their neighbors will lose or win in the great game. Don't tell me! I've seen them do it, and if I dared I'd have startled every soul of them with a rousing peal. Ah, they don't dream whose eye is on them, they never guess what secrets the telegraph wires tell as the messages fly by, and little know what a report I give to the winds of heaven as I ring out above them morning, noon, and night." And the old spirit shook his head till the tassel on his cap jangled like a little bell.

"There are some, however, whom I love and honor," he said, in a benignant tone, "who honestly earn their bread, who deserve all the success that comes to them, and always keep a warm corner in their noble hearts for those less blest than they. These are the men who serve the city in times of peace, save it in times of war, deserve the highest honors in its gift, and leave behind them a record that keeps their memories green. For such an one we lately tolled a knell, my brothers; and as our united voices pealed over the city, in all grateful hearts, sweeter and more solemn than any chime, rung the words that made him so beloved,—

"'Treat our dead boys tenderly, and send them home to me.'"

He ceased, and all the spirits reverently uncovered their gray heads as a strain of music floated up from the sleeping city and died among the stars.

"Like yours, my report is not satisfactory in all respects," began the second spirit, who wore a very pointed cap and a finely ornamented cloak. But, though his dress was fresh and youthful, his face was old, and he had nodded several times during his brother's speech. "My greatest affliction during the past year has been the terrible extravagance which prevails. My post, as you know, is at the court end of the city, and I see all the fashionable vices and follies. It is a marvel to me how so many of these immortal creatures, with such opportunities for usefulness, self-improvement and genuine happiness can be content to go round and round in one narrow circle of unprofitable and unsatisfactory pursuits. I do my best to warn them; Sunday after Sunday I chime in their ears the beautiful old hymns that sweetly chide or cheer the hearts that truly listen and believe; Sunday after Sunday I look down on them as they pass in, hoping to see that my words have not fallen upon deaf ears; and Sunday after Sunday they listen to words that should teach them much, yet seem to go by them like the wind. They are told to love their neighbor, yet too many hate him because he possesses more of this world's goods or honors than they: they are told that a rich man cannot enter the kingdom of heaven, yet they go on laying up perishable wealth, and though often warned that moth and rust will corrupt, they fail to believe it till the worm that destroys enters and mars their own chapel of ease. Being a spirit, I see below external splendor and find much poverty of heart and soul under the velvet and the ermine which should cover rich and royal natures. Our city saints walk abroad in threadbare suits, and under quiet bonnets shine the eyes that make sunshine in the shady places. Often as I watch the glittering procession passing to and fro below me. I wonder if, with all our progress, there is to-day as much real piety as in the times when our fathers, poorly clad, with weapon in one hand and Bible in the other, came weary distances to worship in the wilderness with fervent faith unquenched by danger, suffering and solitude.

"Yet in spite of my fault-finding I love my children, as I call them, for all are not butterflies. Many find wealth no temptation to forgetfulness of duty or hardness of heart. Many give freely of their abundance, pity the poor, comfort the afflicted, and make our city loved and honored in other lands as in our own. They have their cares, losses, and heartaches as well as the poor; it isn't all sunshine with them, and they learn, poor souls, that

"'Into each life some rain must fall,
Some days must be dark and dreary.'

"But I've hopes of them, and lately they have had a teacher so genial, so gifted, so well-beloved that all who listen to him must be better for the lessons of charity, good-will and cheerfulness which he brings home to them by the magic of tears and smiles. We know him, we love him, we always remember him as the year comes round, and the blithest song our brazen tongues utter is a Christmas carol to the Father of 'The Chimes!'"

As the spirit spoke his voice grew cheery, his old face shone, and in a burst of hearty enthusiasm he flung up his cap and cheered like a boy. So did the others, and as the fairy shout echoed through the belfry a troop of shadowy figures, with faces lovely or grotesque, tragical or gay, sailed by on the wings of the wintry wind and waved their hands to the spirits of the bells.

As the excitement subsided and the spirits re-seated themselves, looking ten years younger for that burst, another spoke. A venerable brother in a dingy mantle, with a tuneful voice, and eyes that seemed to have grown sad with looking on much misery.

"He loves the poor, the man we've just hur-rahed for, and he makes others love and remem-ber them, bless him!" said the spirit. "I hope he'll touch the hearts of those who listen to him here and beguile them to open their hands to my un-happy children over yonder. If I could set some of the forlorn souls in my parish beside the happier creatures who weep over imaginary woes as they are painted by his eloquent lips, that brilliant scene would be better than any sermon. Day and night I look down on lives as full of sin, self-sacrifice and suffering as any in those famous books. Day and night I try to comfort the poor by my cheery voice, and to make their wants known by proclaiming them with all my might. But people seem to be so intent on business, pleasure or home duties that they have no time to hear and answer my appeal. There's a deal of charity in this good city, and when the people do wake up they work with a will; but I can't help thinking that if some of the money lavished on luxuries was spent on neces-saries for the poor, there would be fewer tragedies like that which ended yesterday. It's a short story, easy to tell, though long and hard to live; listen to it.

"Down yonder in the garret of one of the squalid houses at the foot of my tower, a little girl has lived for a year, fighting silently and single-handed a good fight against poverty and sin. I saw her when she first came, a hopeful, cheerful, brave-hearted little soul, alone, yet not afraid. She used to sit all day sewing at her window, and her lamp burnt far into the night, for she was very poor, and all she earned would barely give her food and shelter. I watched her feed the doves, who seemed to be her only friends; she never forgot them, and daily gave them the few crumbs that fell from her meagre table. But there was no kind hand to feed and foster the little human dove, and so she starved.

"For a while she worked bravely, but the poor three dollars a week would not clothe and feed and warm her, though the things her busy fingers made sold for enough to keep her comfortably if she had received it. I saw the pretty color fade from her cheeks; her eyes grew hollow, her voice lost its cheery ring, her step its elasticity, and her face began to wear the haggard, anxious look that made its youth doubly pathetic. Her poor little gowns grew shabby, her shawl so thin she shivered when the pitiless wind smote her, and her feet were almost bare. Rain and snow beat on the patient little figure going to and fro, each morning with hope and courage faintly shining, each evening with the shadow of despair gathering darker round her. It was a hard time for all, desperately hard for her, and in her poverty, sin and pleasure tempted her. She resisted, but as another bitter winter came she feared that in her misery she might yield, for body and soul were weakened now by the long struggle. She knew not where to turn for help; there seemed to be no place for her at any safe and happy fireside; life's hard aspect daunted her, and she turned to death, saying confidingly, 'Take me while I'm innocent and not afraid to go.'

"I saw it all! I saw how she sold everything that would bring money and paid her little debts to the utmost penny; how she set her poor room in order for the last time; how she tenderly bade the doves good-by, and lay down on her bed to die. At nine o'clock last night as my bell rang over the city, I tried to tell what was going on in the garret where the light was dying out so fast. I cried to them with all my strength.—

"'Kind souls, below there! a fellow-creature is perishing for lack of charity! Oh, help her before it is too late! Mothers, with little daughters on your knees, stretch out your hands and take her in! Happy women, in the safe shelter of home, think of her desolation! Rich men, who grind the faces of the poor, remember that this soul will one day be required of you! Dear Lord, let not this little sparrow fall to the ground! Help, Christian men and women, in the name of Him whose birth-day blessed the world!'

"Ah me! I rang, and clashed, and cried in vain. The passers-by only said, as they hurried home, laden with Christmas cheer: 'The old bell is merry to-night, as it should be at this blithe season, bless it!'

"As the clocks struck ten, the poor child lay

down, saying, as she drank the last bitter draught life could give her, 'It's very cold, but soon I shall not feel it'; and with her quiet eyes fixed on the cross that glimmered in the moonlight above me, she lay waiting for the sleep that needs no lullaby.

"As the clock struck eleven, pain and poverty for her were over. It was bitter cold, but she no longer felt it. She lay serenely sleeping, with tired heart and hands, at rest forever. As the clocks struck twelve, the dear Lord remembered her, and with fatherly hand led her into the home where there is room for all. To-day I rung her knell, and though my heart was heavy, yet my soul was glad; for in spite of all her human woe and weakness, I am sure that little girl will keep a joyful Christmas up in heaven."

In the silence which the spirits for a moment kept, a breath of softer air than any from the snowy world below swept through the steeple and seemed to whisper, "Yes!"

"Avast there! Fond as I am of salt water, I don't like this kind," cried the breezy voice of the fourth spirit, who had a tiny ship instead of a tassel on his cap, and who wiped his wet eyes with the sleeve of his rough blue cloak. "It won't take me long to spin my yarn; for things are pretty taut and ship-shape aboard our craft. Captain Taylor is an experienced sailor, and has brought many a ship safely into port in spite of wind and tide, and the devil's own whirlpools and hurricanes. If you want to see earnestness come aboard some Sunday when the Captain's on the quarter-deck, and take an observation. No danger of falling asleep there, no more than there is up aloft, 'when the stormy winds do blow.' Consciences get raked fore and aft, sins are blown clean out of the water, false colors are hauled down and true ones run up to the masthead, and many an immortal soul is warned to steer off in time from the pirates, rocks and quicksands of temptation. He's a regular revolving light, is the Captain—a beacon always burning and saying plainly, 'Here are life-boats, ready to put off in all weathers and bring the ship-wrecked into quiet waters.' He comes but seldom now, being laid up in the home dock, tranquilly waiting till his turn comes to go out with the tide and safely ride at anchor in the great harbor of the Lord. Our crew varies a good deal. Some of 'em have rather rough voyages, and come into port pretty well battered; land-sharks fall foul of a good many, and do a deal of damage; but most of 'em carry brave and tender hearts under the blue jackets, for their rough nurse, the sea, manages to keep something of the child alive in the grayest old tar that makes the world his picture-book. We try to supply 'em with life-preservers while at sea, and make 'em feel sure of a hearty welcome when ashore, and I believe the year '67 will sail away into eternity with a satisfactory cargo. Brother North-End made me pipe my eye; so I'll make him laugh to pay for it, by telling a clerical joke I heard the other day. Bellows didn't make it, though he might have done so, as he's a connection of ours, and knows how to use his tongue as well as any of us. Speaking of the bells of a certain town, a reverend gentleman affirmed that each bell uttered an appropriate remark so plainly, that the words were audible to all. The Baptist bell cried, briskly, 'Come up and be dipped! Come up and be dipped!'

The Episcopal bell slowly said, 'Apos-tol-ic suc-cess-ion! Apos-tol-ic suc-cess-ion!' The Orthodox bell solemnly pronounced, 'Eternal damnation! Eternal damnation!' and the Methodist shouted, invitingly, 'Room for all! room for all!'"

As the spirit imitated the various calls, as only a jovial bell-sprite could, the others gave him a chime of laughter, and vowed they would each adopt some tuneful summons, which should reach human ears and draw human feet more willingly to church.

"Faith, brother, you've kept your word and got the laugh out of us," cried a stout, sleek spirit, with a kindly face, and a row of little saints round his cap and a rosary at his side. "It's very well we are doing this year; the cathedral is full, the flock increasing, and the true faith holding its own entirely. Ye may shake your heads if you will and fear there'll be trouble, but I doubt it. We've warm hearts of our own, and the best of us don't forget that when we were starving, America—the saints bless the jewel!—sent us bread; when we were dying for lack of work, America opened her arms and took us in, and now helps us to build churches, homes and schools by giving us a share of the riches all men work for and win. It's a generous nation ye are, and a brave one, and we showed our gratitude by fighting for ye in the day of trouble and giving ye our Phil, and many another broth of a boy. The land is wide enough for us both, and while we work and fight and grow together, each may learn something from the other. I'm free to confess that your religion looks a bit cold and hard to me, even here in the good city where each man may ride his own hobby to death, and hoot at his neighbors as much as he will. You seem to keep your piety shut up all the week in your bare, white churches, and only let it out on Sundays, just a trifle musty with disuse. You set your rich, warm and soft to the fore, and leave the poor shivering at the door. You give your people bare walls to look upon, commonplace music to listen to, dull sermons to put them asleep, and then wonder why they stay away, or take no interest when they come.

"We leave our doors open day and night; our

lamps are always burning, and we may come into our Father's house at any hour. We let rich and poor kneel together, all being equal there. With us abroad you'll see prince and peasant side by side, school-boy and bishop, market-woman and noble lady, saint and sinner, praying to the Holy Mary, whose motherly arms are open to high and low. We make our churches inviting with immortal music, pictures by the world's great masters, and rites that are splendid symbols of the faith we hold. Call it mummery if ye like, but let me ask you why so many of your sheep stray into our fold? It's because they miss the warmth, the hearty, the maternal tenderness which all souls love and long for, and fail to find in your stern, Puritanical belief. By Saint Peter! I've seen many a lukewarm worshipper, who for years has nodded in your cushioned pews, wake and glow with something akin to genuine piety while kneeling on the stone pavement of one of our cathedrals, with Raphael's angels before his eyes, with strains of magnificent music in his ears, and all about him, in shapes of power or beauty, the saints and martyrs who have saved the world, and whose presence inspires him to follow their divine example. It's not complaining of ye I am, but just reminding ye that men are but children after all, and need more tempting to virtue than they do to vice, which last comes easy to 'em since the Fall. Do your best in your own ways to get the poor souls into bliss, and good luck to ye. But remember, there's room in the Holy Mother Church for all, and when your own priests send ye to the divil, come straight to us and we'll take ye in."

"A truly Catholic welcome, bull and all," said the sixth spirit, who, in spite of his old-fashioned garments, had a youthful face, earnest, fearless eyes, and an energetic voice that woke the echoes with its vigorous tones. "I've a hopeful report, brothers, for the reforms of the day are wheeling into rank and marching on. The war isn't over nor rebeldom conquered yet, but the Old Guard has been 'up and at 'em' through the year. There has been some hard fighting, rivers of ink have flowed, and the Washington dawdlers have signalized themselves by a 'masterly inactivity.' The political campaign has been an anxious one; some of the leaders have deserted; some been mustered out; some have fallen gallantly, and as yet have received no monuments. But at the Grand Review the Cross of the Legion of Honor will surely shine on many a brave breast that won no decoration but its virtue here; for the world's fanatics make heaven's heroes, poets say.

"The flock of Nightingales that flew South during the 'winter of our discontent' are all at home again, some here and some in Heaven. But the music of their womanly heroism still lingers in the nation's memory, and makes a tender minor-chord in the battle-hymn of freedom.

"The reform in literature isn't as vigorous as I could wish; but a sharp attack of mental and moral dyspepsia will soon teach *our* people that French confectionery and the bad pastry of Wood, Bracdon, Yates & Co. is not the best diet for the rising generation.

"Speaking of the rising generation reminds me of the schools. They are doing well; they always are, and we are justly proud of them. There may be a slight tendency toward placing too much value upon book-learning; too little upon home culture. Our girls are acknowledged to be uncommonly pretty, witty and wise, but some of us wish they had more health and less excitement, more domestic accomplishments and fewer ologies and isms, and were contented with simple pleasures and the old-fashioned virtues, and not quite so fond of the fast, frivolous life that makes them old so soon. I am fond of our girls and boys. I love to ring for their christenings and marriages, to toll proudly for the brave lads in blue, and tenderly for the innocent creatures whose seats are empty under my old roof. I want to see them anxious to make Young America a model of virtue, strength and beauty, and I believe they will in time.

"There have been some important revivals in religion; for the world won't stand still, and we must keep pace or be left behind to fossilize. A free nation must have a religion broad enough to embrace all mankind, deep enough to fathom and fill the human soul, high enough to reach the source of all love and wisdom, and pure enough to satisfy the wisest and the best. Alarm bells have been rung, anathemas pronounced, and Christians, forgetful of their creed, have abused one another heartily. But the truth always triumphs in the end, and whoever sincerely believes, works and waits for it, by whatever name he calls it, will surely find his own faith blessed to him in proportion to his charity for the faith of others.

"But look!—the first red streaks of dawn are in the East. Our vigil is over, and we must fly home to welcome in the holidays. Before we part, join with me, brothers, in resolving that through the coming year we will with all our hearts and tongues,—

> "'Ring out the old, ring in the new,
> Ring out the false, ring in the true;
> Ring in the valiant man and free,
> Ring in the Christ that is to be.'"

Then hand in hand the spirits of the bells floated away, singing in the hush of dawn the sweet song the stars sung over Bethlehem,— "Peace on earth, good will to men."

POEMS

CHRISTINA ROSETTI

1830-1894

EPIPHANY

"Lord Babe, if Thou art He
We sought for patiently,
Where is Thy court?
Hither may prophecy and star resort;
Men heed not their report."—
"Bow down and worship,
    righteous man:
This Infant of a span
Is He man sought for since the world
    began!"—

"Then, Lord, accept my gold, too base a
    thing
For Thee, of all kings King."—

"Lord Babe, despite Thy youth
I hold Thee of a truth
Both Good and Great:
But wherefore dost Thou keep so mean
    a state,
Low-lying desolate?"—
"Bow down and worship, righteous seer:
The Lord our God is here
Approachable, Who bids us all
    draw near."—
"Wherefore to Thee I offer frankincense,
Thou Sole Omnipotence."—

"But I have only brought
Myrrh; no wise afterthought
Instructed me
To gather pearls or gems, or choice to see
Coral or ivory."—

"Not least thine offering proves
    thee wise:
For myrrh means sacrifice,
And He that lives, this Same is He
    that dies."—
"Then here is myrrh: alas, yea woe is me
That myrrh befitteth Thee."—

Myrrh, frankincense, and gold:
And lo from wintry fold
Good-will doth bring
A Lamb, the innocent likeness of this King
Whom stars and seraphs sing:
And lo the bird of love, a Dove,
Flutters and coos above:
And Dove and Lamb and Babe agree
    in love:—
Come all mankind, come all creation
    hither,
Come, worship Christ together.

THE SHEPHERDS HAD AN ANGEL

The shepherds had an angel,
The wise men had a star;
But what have I, a little child,
To guide me home from far,
Where glad stars sing together,
And singing angels are?

Lord Jesus is my Guardian,
So I can nothing lack;
The lambs lie in His bosom
Along life's dangerous track:
The willful lambs that go astray
He, bleeding, brings them back.

Those shepherds thro' the lonely night
Sat watching by their sheep,
Until they saw the heav'nly host
Who neither tire nor sleep,
All singing Glory, glory,
In festival they keep.

Christ watches me, His little lamb,
Cares for me day and night,
That I may be His own in heav'n;
So angels clad in white
Shall sing their Glory, glory,
For my sake in the height.

Lord, bring me nearer day by day,
Till I my voice unite,
And sing my Glory, glory,
With angels clad in white.
All Glory, glory, giv'n to Thee,
Thro' all the heav'nly height.

NAHUM TATE

1652-1715

WHILE SHEPHERDS WATCHED THEIR FLOCKS BY NIGHT

While shepherds watched their flocks by
    night,
All seated on the ground,
The angel of the Lord came down,
And glory shone around.

"Fear not," said he (for mighty dread
Had seized their troubled mind;)
"Glad tidings of great joy I bring
To you and all mankind.

"To you, in David's town this day
Is born of David's line
The Saviour, who is Christ the Lord;
And this shall be the sign.

"The Heavenly Babe you there shall find
To human view displayed,
All meanly wrapt in swathing bands,
And in a manger laid."

Thus spake the Seraph; and forthwith
Appeared a shining throng
Of angels, praising God, and thus
Addressed their joyful song:

"All glory be to God on high,
And to the earth be peace;
Good will henceforth from Heaven
        to men
Begin, and never cease!"

WILLIAM CULLEN BRYANT

1794-1878

THE STAR OF BETHLEHEM

As shadows cast by cloud and sun,
Flit o'er the summer grass,
So, in thy sight, Almighty One!
Earth's generations pass.

And while the years, an endless host,
Come pressing swiftly on,
The brightest names that earth can boast
Just glisten, and are gone.

Yet doth the star of Bethlehem shed
A lustre pure and sweet;

And still it leads, as once it led,
To the Messiah's feet.

O Father, may that holy star
Grow every year more bright,
And send its glorious beams afar
To fill the world with light.

CHRISTMAS IN 1875

No trumpet-blast profaned
The hour in which the Prince of Peace
    was born;
No bloody streamlet stained
Earth's silver rivers on that sacred morn;
But, o'er the peaceful plain,
The war-horse drew the peasant's
    loaded wain.

The soldier had laid by
The sword and stripped the corselet from
    his breast,
And hung his helm on high—

The sparrow's winter home and
    summer nest;
And, with the same strong hand
That flung the barbèd spear, he tilled
    the land.

Oh, time for which we yearn;
Oh, sabbath of the nations long foretold!
Season of peace, return,
Like a late summer when the year
    grows old,
When the sweet sunny days
Steeped mead and mountain-side in
    golden haze.

For now two rival kings
Flaunt, o'er our bleeding land, their
    hostile flags,
And every sunrise brings
The hovering vulture from his
    mountain-crags
To where the battle-plain

Is strewn with dead, the youth and
    flower of Spain.

Christ is not come, while yet
O'er half the earth the threat of battle
    lowers,
And our own fields are wet,
Beneath the battle-cloud, with crimson
    showers—
The life-blood of the slain,
Poured out where thousands die that one
    may reign.

Soon, over half the earth,
In every temple crowds shall kneel
    again
To celebrate His birth
Who brought the message of good-will
    to men,
And bursts of joyous song
Shall shake the roof above the prostrate
    throng.

Christ is not come, while there
The men of blood whose crimes affront
    the skies
Kneel down in act of prayer,
Amid the joyous strains, and when they
    rise
Go forth, with sword and flame,
To waste the land in His most
    holy name.

Oh, when the day shall break
O'er realms unlearned in warfare's
    cruel arts,
And all their millions wake
To peaceful tasks performed with loving
    hearts,
On such a blessed morn,
Well may the nations say that Christ
    is born.

MARGARET DELAND

1857-1945

THE CHRISTMAS SILENCE

Hushed are the pigeons cooing low,
On dusty rafters of the loft;
And mild-eyed oxen, breathing soft,
Sleep on the fragrant hay below.

Dim shadows in the corner hide;
The glimmering lantern's rays are shed
Where one young lamb just lifts
　　his head,
Then huddles 'gainst his mother's side.

Strange silence tingles in the air;
Through the half-open door a bar

Of light from one low hanging star
Touches a baby's radiant hair—

No sound—the mother, kneeling, lays
Her cheek against the little face.
Oh human love! Oh heavenly grace!
'Tis yet in silence that she prays!

Ages of silence end to-night;
Then to the long-expectant earth
Glad angels come to greet His birth
In burst of music, love, and light!

GEORGE MACDONALD

1824-1905

MARY'S SONG

Babe Jesus lay in Mary's lap;
The sun shone in his hair;
And this was how she saw, mayhap,
The crown already there.

For she sang: "Sleep on, my little king,
Bad Herod dares not come;
Before thee sleeping, holy thing,
The wild winds would be dumb.

"I kiss thy hands, I kiss thy feet,
My child, so long desired;

Thy hands will never be soiled, my
    sweet;
Thy feet will never be tired.

"For thou art the king of men, my son;
Thy crown I see it plain!
And men shall worship thee, every one,
And cry, Glory! Amen!"

Babe Jesus opened his eyes so wide!
At Mary looked her Lord.
Mother Mary stinted her song and
    sighed.
Babe Jesus said never a word.